WraithTalkers
and the
Secret of the Red Monk

D H Chitson

Copyright 2011-22 by D H Chitson

This novel is a work of fiction. Names, characters, places and incidents are all products of the author's imagination. Any resemblance to actual events, locales or persons, living or dead (or somewhere in-between) is entirely coincidental.

All rights reserved.

No part of this publication can be reproduced or transmitted in any form by any means, electronic or mechanical, without permission in writing by D H Chitson.

20226020

Titles in the WraithTalkers Mystery Series:

1. *WraithTalkers and the Secret of the Red Monk*
2. *WraithTalkers and the Mystery of the Singing Mermaid*
3. *WraithTalkers and the Secret of Hathaway Hall*
4. *WraithTalkers and the Mystery of Lacheoch Island*
5. *WraithTalkers and the Adventure of Nightshade Lodge*
6. *WraithTalkers and the Demon of Derwyddon*
7. *WraithTalkers and the Curse of the Green Dragon*

This book is dedicated to George

"Faithless is he that says farewell when the road darkens."
J.R.R. Tolkien

Contents

DOCTOR BLACK	1
THE MYSTERIOUS BOX	12
THE INSTITUTE	24
THE CHURCH	38
GHOSTS	53
THE SPIRIT	70
THE KEY	84
THE RED MONK	100
REVELATIONS	116
ZARATHUSTRA	129
THE SECRET	148

DOCTOR BLACK

Marigold Bennett was the cleverest and bravest person that Gideon knew. He was thinking this as he watched his sister screw the lid back onto a little glass jar into which she had just collected some pond water. Marigold had slid along a precarious branch that overhung the pond, purely to collect a sample from a "quiet corner" of the slime-covered water.

"Come on Giddy, let's get this home and under the microscope!" declared Marigold.

Giddy was Marigold's affectionate name for her smaller brother. She would always use this name when there was just the two of them, however in public she would usually call him Gideon to avoid his embarrassment.

"Do you think we'll see any little creepy-crawlies?" asked Gideon.

"I'm not sure. We should do, although I might have to wind up the magnification a bit."

The two children trekked away from Blackthorn Pond, back down the path they had used a few minutes earlier. Any outside observer watching the pair of them re-enter the housing estate at the edge of Avonmead, a sleepy town in the leafy English county of Warwickshire, would easily guess that Marigold and Gideon were brother and sister. Both were thin and small for their age but the obvious physical similarity, the one that everyone noticed, was that they each had thick, fiery ginger hair.

Marigold, at thirteen years of age, was three years older than her brother. She had clear emerald eyes that contrasted beautifully with her hair, a slightly upturned nose, like her father's she had been told, and a sprinkling of freckles that darkened in the sun. Marigold often tied her thick shoulder-length hair back into a little bunch but today it was hanging loose in a rather untidy fashion.

Marigold always seemed to have her upturned nose in a book. Her favourite reading material was mystery fiction, especially the Sherlock Holmes stories. Although considered to be old-fashioned and stuffy by many of her friends, Marigold loved the fact that the mysteries were set in the bygone era of Victorian London, and she was always thrilled at Sherlock Holmes' intellectual prowess and powers of deduction. Marigold's mother often used to joke that for her eighteenth birthday she was going to buy Marigold two of Sherlock Holmes' most treasured possessions: a pipe and a violin!

Gideon usually walked around with a serious expression on his face. This wasn't because he was a serious boy; it was more to do with the fact that he had grown up never wanting to appear stupid in his sister's company. For most of his life, Gideon had felt as if he'd lived in his sister's shadow. She was much cleverer and confident than he was. Somehow he felt that he had to concentrate the whole time he was with her. Gideon also had freckles, although not nearly as many as Marigold. His messy red hair was always in a state of permanent explosion.

The two siblings were not far from home now. The day was the hottest of the summer so far and both children were in shorts and flimsy T-shirts. There wasn't a cloud in the sky. The grey pavement was baking hot and constantly warmed the children's bare legs as they walked along.

"Phew, I shall be glad to get a juice," declared Marigold. "I'm almost tempted to sip at this pond water!"

Gideon smiled at his sister. He was just about to reply when something stopped the children in their tracks. They had turned a corner and were passing an old red brick house. The detached and imposing building was unusual in that it was older than the surrounding houses, and about twice their size.

Fields had probably surrounded it at one time before the estate grew up to lap against its boundary.

But it wasn't the building that had stopped the children; it was the scream! It wasn't the sort of scream of someone banging his thumb with a hammer. It wasn't the scream of someone being angry with someone else. It wasn't even the scream of someone who had just been surprised. Marigold thought that it was the scream of someone who was in very, very great pain!

"It's coming from that house!" exclaimed Marigold.

Gideon didn't say anything. His face was more serious than ever as he wondered what could have caused someone to call out like that.

Marigold had a quick look around. The two children were alone in the street. "Come on Giddy," she commanded, and before Gideon could properly react, his sister had jumped over the low wall that ran along the side of the house and was making her way around to the front. Gideon felt compelled to follow.

Marigold banged on the door. Before waiting for a reply, she noticed a brass doorknocker and gave that a few 'rat-tat-tats' too. The children waited for a few seconds and Marigold put down the jar of pond water she had been carrying. There were no more screams. There was not a sound from inside the house. All that could be heard was a lone bee buzzing amongst the warm, colourful flowers of the front garden.

The urgency started to rise in Marigold. She gave the door another few bangs. Almost immediately she decided she was going to go round the back and dashed off without a word.

"But Marigold …" called Gideon after his sister, but he knew it was no use. He gave his shoulders a shrug and gave chase.

Gideon was used to Marigold acting on her instincts. She had been known as 'Marigold the Bold' within the family for as long as he could remember. In fact his earliest recollection was standing in the large back garden of his Grandparent's house, watching the young Marigold climbing what seemed to be the tallest tree in the world. Halfway up Marigold had lost her footing and had come crashing to the ground with a dull thud. Gideon had instinctively rushed over to his sister's side, but she had got up immediately, fighting back the tears. Gideon, half frozen with fear, had to look on helplessly as Marigold went back to the trunk and started climbing again. The next time she made it.

At the back of the house Marigold was alternately stepping back to look at the bedroom windows above and stepping forward to bang on the back door. She had already tried the handle and it was locked.

"Shouldn't we just leave it, Marigold?" said Gideon in a feeble sort of voice, as if he knew what the response was going to be. Marigold gave him a look that was both of exasperation and of anger.

"Let's call the police or an ambulance," Gideon pleaded, feeling an all-too-common sense of frustration with his sister.

"I'm going up," Marigold replied, and Gideon watched helplessly as his sister began to climb a cast-iron drainpipe fixed next to the back door.

It only took a second for Gideon to realise that Marigold was heading towards the only open window at the back of the house. The opening at the bottom appeared to be wide enough for a small person to slip through, although nothing of the inside could be seen because the curtains were tightly drawn. It dawned on Gideon that the scream had probably emanated from the gap in the window. This was something that Marigold had already deduced.

Marigold climbed the drainpipe with the demeanour of an excited monkey. Perhaps she was a little too quick, for at the halfway point she momentarily lost her footing and for one terrifying instant it looked as if she was going to plunge hideously back to the ground. Gideon's heart leapt as Marigold's feet scraped frantically against the brickwork. His mind immediately went back to the time he had seen his sister fall from the tree. Fortunately Marigold's trainers quickly bit into the wall and the agile girl continued upwards, reaching the open window without further incident. Marigold hauled the top half of her body over the window ledge, before rolling forward into the house and out of sight. Gideon let out a huge sigh of relief. He realised he'd been holding his breath ever since Marigold had started the climb.

Once inside, it took a few moments for Marigold's eyes to get accustomed to the darkness. She glanced around and quickly realised that she was in a bedroom. An open doorway was visible in the opposite wall, over in the far corner from where she was standing. A double bed blocked her direct path to the door. The blankets had mostly been pulled off the bed and they appeared to be lying in a heap on the floor space that was furthest from Marigold. Apart from this, the room looked very tidy. A long dressing table with a mirror stood against the right-hand wall. On the dressing table were placed a hairbrush, a few toiletries and a china vase. To the right of Marigold, beside the window, a large wooden wardrobe loomed. Marigold jumped. *'What's that?'* she thought, as she stared at the space beyond the wardrobe. But it was only its shadow, shimmering slightly in the dappled light.

After getting access to the house so quickly, Marigold now felt decidedly uncomfortable. She was in someone else's house, with no real reason for being there other than believing that someone was in trouble. Marigold decided against calling out and stood still for a few seconds more, listening. She heard nothing, until a slightly muffled "Marigold!" reached her ears. It was Gideon from below. Marigold threw back the curtains and leaned out of the window.

"Wait there, Giddy! It all seems quiet up here. I'm going to have a look around."

Gideon nodded.

With the curtains drawn back and the bedroom now filled with bright light, Marigold took another look around. What she had not noticed before was a small table on the far side of the bed, near to the door. It had an old-fashioned telephone on it with a taut cord leading down to the bundle of blankets. It appeared as if the handset was somehow tangled up with the mess on the floor.

With rising anxiety, Marigold inched around the foot of the bed to get a better look. As she did so, she found that she couldn't take her eyes from the blankets as they slowly crept into full view.

Marigold's heart gave a little jump. There was someone tangled up in the mess! She couldn't see the person's face, but the general outline seemed to be that of a man. Marigold felt as if a hundred butterflies had been released inside her stomach. She looked at the scene before her. The body wasn't moving now, but whoever it was had obviously tried to grab the blankets for support, probably to get back onto the bed. He had only succeeded in pulling them down on top of himself. In one hand he held the telephone receiver.

Marigold did the only thing she could think of. "Hello?" she said, rather softly and nervously.

There was no answer. The man didn't move.

Breathing deeply and gathering up her courage, Marigold moved closer and very carefully pulled back the corner of blanket that was covering his face. Immediately she had done this she wished that she hadn't: the face was horribly and hideously contorted! It was obvious that the man had been in very, very great pain. Some sort of yellowish liquid still trickled slowly out of the corner of his mouth. Both eyes were open, but they had rolled completely back in his head, giving him a rather frightening appearance. Marigold had never seen a dead person before; however, she instinctively knew that this man was most definitely not alive! She had read literally hundreds of detective and mystery stories in her young life, including the complete works of her beloved Sherlock Holmes. Dead bodies had popped up all over the place, but when she was confronted with someone who was *genuinely* dead, it was very, very different. This wasn't entertainment. She couldn't just close the pages and walk away. This dead man was real.

Although the body was completely lifeless, she still felt an instinct to check it. She decided to feel for a pulse but first she wanted to see if the body was still warm. She was sure that she'd seen someone doing this on television.

Ever so slowly she moved the back of her hand towards the man's cheek. It was the one furthest away from the horrible-looking yellow liquid. Closer… closer… her hand was almost there. Marigold looked at the blank eyes in front of her. She suddenly had a feeling they were going to roll back and look at her. Closer, closer and… touch! Marigold sensed that the cheek was still warm.

BANG! BANG! BANG! Marigold leapt away from the body and gave a shriek. She found herself shaking so much she thought she was going to collapse. Somehow she managed to swallow the lump that appeared to have leapt up into her throat from her stomach. It only took a second for her to realise that the body hadn't moved. The man still lay there with his eyes rolled back and the yellow liquid still forming a trail down from the corner of his mouth. Marigold's mind was racing. What was that noise? After a couple of deep breaths, she realised that someone had been banging on the front door. It must be Gideon! What was he doing there? She leapt to the window and looked out, but Gideon was still down below at the back of the house, looking up. With a tingling, Marigold darted out of the bedroom and onto a long dark landing. Without stopping, she worked out which door would lead to a bedroom at the front of the house and she ran through it. She found herself in a smaller room than the bedroom she'd just been in. Marigold had just time to notice a neat single bed with a rose-patterned quilt on it before she was at the front window. The window had net curtains, which she knew would give her some protection from anybody looking up at the house from the outside. Marigold peered out.

A large black Mercedes Benz car was parked directly outside. She knew it was a Mercedes because a friend of her mother had a similar car. Marigold also knew that the car hadn't been there when she and Gideon had walked past a few minutes ago. Standing by the car, on the pavement directly outside the house, were two large men. They were both wearing smart dark suits and wrap-around sunglasses. Their gaze was fixed on the front of the house and Marigold stood on tiptoe to try to see what they were looking at. She was careful not to brush the net curtains with her head; she didn't want any ripples acting as a signal to the men below.

BANG! BANG! BANG! There were two *other* men who were at the front door! From what she could make out, looking down almost onto the tops of their heads, these other men were *also* wearing dark suits and wrap-around sunglasses.

One of the men at the door called out. "DOCTOR BLACK!"

The deep strong-sounding voice frightened Marigold a little. It sounded as if these men meant business.

She suddenly remembered Gideon! When those men couldn't get into the front of the house, they were sure to come around the back! Marigold raced back through the house to the rear bedroom. She skipped round the body, which had still not moved, and leant out of the window.

"Giddy!" she hissed, in a voice that was a form of stifled shout.

Gideon, who was still looking up at the window, was now bouncing up and down and pointing at the house with some urgency, as if he had also heard the banging and calling.

Marigold made a split-second assessment of the situation. She knew that Gideon couldn't easily climb the drainpipe she had used earlier, and anyway what was the sense in the two of them being trapped? She also knew that Gideon couldn't return around the side of the house; he would undoubtedly run into the men at the front! No, Marigold realised that Gideon must hide somewhere in the back garden, and from her high vantage point she knew just where.

"Get between the shed and the fence and hide! QUICKLY! Someone's coming!"

Gideon acted immediately, darting to where Marigold was frantically pointing: a small gap between a small garden tool shed and the high fence that completely encircled the rear garden.

Marigold started to think about climbing down the drainpipe, but any thoughts that she had about this quickly evaporated when she heard a loud crashing sound. The front door had been violently kicked open! Marigold knew that she had to hide, and she had to do it quickly. She dived for the wardrobe. It was locked! There was no space under the bed. She darted for the open bedroom door and stepped as quietly as she could onto the landing. Downstairs she could hear at least two of the men thumping and banging their way through the downstairs rooms. Marigold looked around frantically. Where could she hide? She would certainly be found in any of the bedrooms. In the gloom of the landing, she noticed that one of the doors had a different handle. It was probably a linen cupboard. Could she squeeze inside? Right in front of the door stood a black leather briefcase. Marigold picked it up as she opened the cupboard. There was just enough room for the small girl to slip inside. There was no handle on the inside of the cupboard door, but Marigold didn't panic. Clutching the briefcase to her chest, and using the fingertips of one hand, she pulled the door towards her as best she could. She was just in time: Marigold heard the muffled sound of heavy footsteps running up the stairs. A split second later someone had reached the landing.

"He's in here!" The leading man had obviously seen the body through the open bedroom door.

Marigold stood and listened from the darkness of the linen cupboard. The door was open by only the tiniest crack, and it was not enough for her to see anything of the men. She held her breath as she tried to work out how many of the men had entered the bedroom. She thought it was four.

"He's dead," said a man with a very deep voice. He had obviously just checked the body. He then said something that sent a chill down Marigold's spine: "Deuteron, search the other rooms. It must be here somewhere. It will be in a black briefcase. You others, help me to move the body onto the bed"

A black briefcase! Marigold's heart jumped. She realised that she was still holding the case she had picked up a few moments earlier! The men would surely discover her feeble hiding place and find her with it. What would she say? Something like *'Uh, hello, I was just passing. Is this what you are after?'* She thought not. These men were big and probably very strong. They were dressed in serious clothes. They thought nothing of breaking down doors to get at what they wanted. They would probably kill her there and then, or perhaps take her away for a bit of torture first!

Marigold closed her eyes and clutched the briefcase even tighter to her chest. She felt as if her pounding heart must surely give her away: it was beating against the briefcase like a drum! She tried to think clearly. Why were the men looking for this briefcase? Did it contain money? Jewellery? It certainly felt quite heavy. Why, oh why had she picked it up? Her thoughts were interrupted by the sound of heavy footsteps on the landing. They arrived at her linen cupboard and Marigold started to feel sick, but, to her great relief, whoever it was stomped straight past. He was going to check the front bedrooms first.

Marigold knew it would only be a matter of time before she was found. She also knew that trying to escape would be very risky. At the moment there were probably three men in the back bedroom and one more in the front. If she was going to attempt to escape Marigold realised that it was now or never.

She slowly pushed open the linen cupboard door. There was no reaction. No shouts of anger. She stepped carefully out... good! Nobody seemed to have noticed. She could hear the man who had just passed her by. He was searching the little bedroom she had looked out from at the front of the house. She could also hear the other men talking, louder now, in the back bedroom. They seemed to be moving the body onto the bed but were having difficulty with all the blankets. Marigold could hardly believe her luck: the bedroom door was half closed! The men must have pushed it to get better access to the body and she was sure she could now walk past without being seen!

Marigold stepped quietly down the landing and for a moment she thought of putting the briefcase down. She knew that the men would find it and she could leave the house and never be troubled again, but something inside her knew this wouldn't be right. She decided to keep the briefcase with her, reasoning that she could always give it back later. Marigold slipped past the bedroom with the men in it. The only thing that would let her down now was a loose floorboard. She was in luck, nothing squeaked, and she hurried silently down the stairs into the hall below. The broken front door was wide open. Splintered wood covered the hall carpet. She was almost free. She ran outside and down the front path.

"STOP!"

Marigold turned towards the muffled yell, just long enough to see a man shouting at her from behind the front bedroom window. He had pulled the net curtains aside and he looked very angry indeed! Marigold didn't stop. She clutched the briefcase to her chest once more and raced as fast as she could down the road, adrenaline coursing through her veins.

After what seemed like a lifetime, although it was probably only a few seconds, she came to the corner of the road and had the courage to look over her shoulder. Nobody was behind her yet, but she knew it wouldn't be long before there would be four angry men spilling out into the street.

Marigold turned the corner, only to run headlong into someone who grabbed her tightly!

THE MYSTERIOUS BOX

Marigold and her captor came crashing down to the ground and the briefcase went flying into the road. Her assailant had lost his grip and had fallen backwards. Marigold raised her head.

"Gideon!" she shouted, mostly out of relief.

"Ouch!" complained Gideon.

"Come on! We must go! There are men after us!"

Marigold scrambled up and took the briefcase by its handle. Gideon was still sat on the pavement, looking hurt.

"Come ON!" urged Marigold.

She grabbed him by the elbow and helped him to his feet. Looking back down the street, Marigold could see that two of the dark-suited men were already in hot pursuit. Gideon had also seen them, and the children sped off down the next avenue.

Although younger than his sister, Gideon was a faster runner. Soon he was pulling away from Marigold, who shouted an instruction: "Take the next alleyway."

Gideon made a sharp left-hand turn and ran up a small alleyway that ran along the side of a house. The alleyway veered to the right and soon Marigold knew that they couldn't be seen from the road.

"Turn right at the end, cross the road and take the next alleyway!"

Gideon followed the instructions to the letter. The children dodged this way and that through the back alleys, all the while making good progress in the general direction of their home. Soon Marigold became convinced that nobody would have been able to follow the maze-like route they had taken. She imagined that perhaps two of the men would have chased them on foot, whilst the other two took the car. Marigold thought it highly likely that the Mercedes would be cruising the streets of the estate, trying to sniff them out.

"Let's stop here for a while," said Marigold, her heart hammering in her chest. The alleyway they were in had a little recess with a household's back gate. The two siblings sat down on a convenient slab and panted heavily.

"What happened to you?" asked Gideon after a while. "I was so worried!"

Marigold filled him in. She told him about the dead body she had found. She told him about the dark-suited men who wore wrap-around sunglasses, and how they had smashed their way into the house. Gideon's eyes widened when Marigold explained how she had hidden in the linen cupboard. She also told him about the black briefcase and how, in her haste, she had taken it into the cupboard with her and how the men seemed to want it so desperately. Marigold described how she had made her escape by creeping down the stairway and running down the road, but not before she had been spotted by one of the men.

Gideon gave a low whistle. "So that's why you looked so scared when you bumped into me!"

"Yes, and what were *you* doing hanging around that corner?"

Gideon quickly told his side of the story, even though it was not half as exciting as Marigold's. He had hidden at the side of the shed, he explained, just as Marigold had wanted him to. He had managed to lie down on the ground and peer round the corner, using a small shrub for cover. He had waited for a while, but nobody had appeared.

"That's because they had smashed down the front door and rushed in," interrupted Marigold.

Gideon nodded. "Yes. They must have been in a terrible hurry!"

He explained how, after some banging that seemed to come from the ground floor, he could hear the faint sounds of the men talking in the bedroom through the open upstairs window. At this point he had started to get worried about Marigold. "I thought that you might be getting into trouble," he said, "so I came out of the hiding place and carefully tiptoed around the front of the house. When I saw the front door smashed in I started to get really scared, I'm sorry, and I ran down the road. I thought that I would run home and get Mum and maybe get her to call the police or something. But when I reached the corner, it was like there was a magnet or something pulling me back. I knew that I shouldn't be leaving you. Then when I came running back, I bumped straight into you!"

Marigold rested her hand on her brother's shoulder. "Thanks, Giddy," she said. "For coming back, I mean."

Gideon smiled and blushed slightly. "That's OK."

Marigold took a deep breath. "We'd better get back home. If you hear a car, dive into the nearest garden and hide."

Fortunately the coast was clear, and the two children managed to reach home without further incident. Their mother was still at work, so they let themselves in using the spare key. As usual it was hidden under the third plant pot on the left.

As children of a single parent, Marigold and Gideon had learned how to be independent at an early age. Since Marigold had turned thirteen, their mother mostly trusted them to look after themselves during holiday times. She knew that Marigold was sensible.

It hadn't always been that way. Marigold had often been a worry to her mother in the past, having certain behavioural traits that were different from many other children. These included her apparent lack of fear, her strong sense of independence, and her preference for being alone. The only exception to the latter was her complete devotion to Gideon. Marigold knew that she was slightly different from other children but considered her personality and abilities to be a gift.

The children's father had left the family home when Gideon was a baby. Neither of the children could remember their father. He apparently now lived in Australia with another woman. Their mother would never talk about him, and the children didn't know why the relationship had broken down. The children had not even seen a photograph of him. Marigold had learned that her nose was like her father's from an older cousin, whom the children had once met at a wedding. The cousin had started to talk about the children's father, until their mother had re-joined them and abruptly changed the topic of conversation.

The pair now sat cross-legged, facing each other in Gideon's bedroom. Marigold had cleaned her knee and had checked Gideon's palms, both of which had got slight grazes from when he had tumbled over in his clash with Marigold.

Between them stood the black briefcase. Marigold's face was shining with excitement. "Giddy, we have a mystery of our own!" she began.

Gideon nodded. He had a serious expression on his face. He knew he was going to have to keep up with Marigold's thinking.

"What I want us to do is to look at the facts, make a few deductions and only then decide what to do," continued Marigold. "It's what Sherlock Holmes would have done."

Gideon looked doubtful. "Maybe, but I think we ought to call the police. All of this dead body stuff is really serious."

Even as he said it, he knew that Marigold would give him a crushing look. She didn't let him down. "It may be that we decide to call the police, but let's not go rushing in," she said, glaring at him. "Let's start at the beginning. There is indeed a dead body. It's also reasonable to assume it's a man called Dr Black, because that is the name that one of the dark-suited men shouted out. We also know that Dr Black died this afternoon, shortly after we heard him scream."

"How do you know it was him that we heard screaming?" asked Gideon. "Perhaps it was some other poor man?"

"No, I don't think so. For one thing we are both sure that the scream came from that open window. Also, Dr Black's cheek was still warm." Marigold chewed on her bottom lip, which was always a sign that her brain was moving up a gear. "We also know that he was probably on the phone to someone when it happened. The most likely explanation is that he was trying to call for an ambulance."

"That's a good point," said Gideon. "For all we know, after we escaped from the house, an ambulance and several police cars might have turned up. Those men in suits might have all been arrested!"

"Hmm, it's possible," said Marigold, chewing her bottom lip. "The truth is, we don't know who or what killed Dr Black. He might have died from a natural cause, but I don't know what natural cause causes your eyes to roll back and yellow stuff to dribble out of your mouth."

"Maybe he was strangled, or stabbed?"

"But that would have meant that someone else would have been in the house."

"Maybe there was!" said Gideon, starting to think that he might get the better of his sister. "You didn't check all of the rooms. Someone else could have been hiding in there, just as you did!"

Marigold hadn't thought of this. She chewed her lip some more. "No, I don't think so. If you were murdering someone you wouldn't let him make a phone call."

"Unless the murderer saw you climbing in the window and got scared!"

Marigold put her head on one side and gave Gideon one of her '*help me constructively or keep quiet*' looks. Gideon pursed his lips together and Marigold went on with her reasoning. "The truth is that we don't have enough medical knowledge to know what killed Dr Black, although I don't think he was stabbed. I'm sure there would have been lots of blood if he had, and I saw none."

Gideon suddenly sat upright. "We might have made a terrible mistake!" he blurted out.

"How do you mean?" said Marigold.

"Those men in dark suits and sunglasses may not be suspicious characters. They could have *been* policemen! Perhaps Dr Black had already made his phone call, and the nearest people who were alerted happened to be four plain clothed officers! The police would certainly smash down a door if they thought someone was ill inside! Perhaps there's a really, really simple explanation to all of this."

Marigold chewed on her lip some more. Gideon looked at her expectantly with a hint of triumph on his face. Had he cracked Marigold's mystery?

"No, I don't think it's that straightforward," said Marigold after a short while, much to Gideon's disappointment. "Policemen wouldn't move a body when the cause of death hasn't been determined. Those men did. But my biggest concern is that they didn't seem to be very interested in Dr Black. They were more concerned with the black briefcase."

Both children stared at the object in front of them.

"Are we going to open it?" asked Gideon.

"Of course," said Marigold, smiling.

Before the children could take any further action, an unexpected ringing of the front doorbell made them both jump.

"It's the police!" cried Gideon. "They've come to arrest us!"

Marigold was already on her feet but her first thoughts were something else: The men in dark suits and wrap-around sunglasses! They must have followed the children home! She cursed herself for being so stupid. She should have led Gideon to safety. Why, oh why hadn't she checked to see if anybody had been following them? Marigold had a sinking feeling as she darted into her mother's front bedroom. There was no escape this time. If the men in dark suits came crashing through the front door the children would be trapped. She stood at the side of her mother's plain front curtains and pressed herself against the wall. She edged over and peered out of the window. She fully expected to see the Black Mercedes Benz car again, looking just as ominous and unwelcome as it had earlier outside Dr Black's house. But to her delight all she could see was her mother's little car.

"Giddy! It's Mum!" shouted Marigold.

Gideon gave a squeal of delight from his back bedroom, and he pushed the black briefcase under his bed. The two children bounded downstairs.

"Hi Mum," said Marigold, as she opened the front door.

"Hi," replied her mother as she fell inside with four bags of heavy shopping. "It's nice to see you two looking so pleased to see me! Where's the spare key? I forgot to take my own this morning."

Marigold realised that she still had the spare key in her pocket. In her haste to get inside earlier she had forgotten to replace it under the flowerpot.

"Sorry Mum," said Marigold, holding up the key. Her mother gave her a smile, and the two children helped to carry the shopping bags through into the kitchen.

Ruth Bennett was a slim woman of average height and a pleasant appearance. Her hair had been the same bright colour as that of her offspring, but thirty-eight years of life had now turned it to a somewhat lighter shade, with just the odd fleck of grey. Ruth's eyes were also a shade lighter than Marigold's: a rather attractive blend of emerald and grey marble.

"Have you two got up to anything interesting today?"

The events of the afternoon flashed briefly across Marigold's mind before she replied. "Not much. We walked up to Blackthorn Pond to collect some water to look at under the microscope."

Marigold suddenly remembered that she'd left the jar of pond water outside Dr Black's house. She hoped that her mother wouldn't ask to see the jar, but she needn't have worried. Her mother was busy putting some items away in the refrigerator and could only manage a "That's nice" in reply.

"Mum," Gideon started to ask.

"Yes dear?"

"When we were walking back from the pond, we noticed the old brick building on the corner of Arden Road."

Marigold glared at her brother. What was he doing? Was he about to tell his mother all that had happened earlier?

In truth Gideon was still feeling a little sore at Marigold getting the better of him in her reasoning about Doctor Black and his possible murder. He thought that asking his mother about the house would be a good idea, but he also knew it would unnerve Marigold.

"What about it, dear?" asked his mother.

"We just wondered who lived in it, as it seems to be such a strange place."

Marigold held her breath. What would her mother say? She half expected her mother to reply: "Well it was alright until someone was murdered there this afternoon," but instead the conversation continued quite normally.

"Dr Black lives there. He used to live with his mother, but she died a couple of years back. He seems to be a lonely sort of fellow. Nobody knows much about him."

Marigold and Gideon exchanged glances. It *was* Dr Black's house!

"Is he one of the doctors at the surgery?" asked Marigold innocently.

"No," replied her mother. "He's not that sort of doctor. He's some sort of scientist at the Hermitage Institute; you know, that place near the woods at the edge of town."

The children knew where the Institute was. You couldn't help but drive past it whenever you left Avonmead by the main road. The building couldn't be seen because it was hidden behind dense trees, but big black letters on a white sign by the side of the drive proclaimed that it was the Hermitage Institute. Thanks to Marigold, when Gideon was much younger, he used to think that a hermit lived there.

"Scientist?" queried Marigold. "What did, I mean does he do?"

"I don't know. I would imagine that it's research into something or other. They seem to investigate all sorts of things at that place."

Marigold thought that she had heard enough for now. She didn't want to spend too long discussing Dr Black. "We were just playing a game upstairs, Mum," she said, anxious to get back upstairs to the briefcase. "Is there anything you want us for at the moment?"

"Nothing for now. I'll finish the unpacking and then I'm going to prepare dinner. I won't need any help tonight; I'll give you a call when it's ready."

Marigold glanced at her watch. That would give them at least an hour of undisturbed time! The children raced upstairs, and Gideon pulled the briefcase out from under his bed.

"Let me do it," said Marigold, and Gideon dutifully handed her the bag. Marigold put her fingers on the single catch. She paused and looked at Gideon straight in the eyes. "If, as I suspect, the case is full of money or jewels," she said solemnly, "we must tell Mum everything and get her to call the police. We must tell the truth and I don't think that we'll get into trouble. I think people will believe that we tried to act for the best."

Gideon nodded and his eyes returned to the case. Marigold undid the catch and the briefcase yawned as she pulled it open.

"What's in it?" said Gideon, barely able to keep still with excitement.

Marigold didn't answer. She reached inside and pulled out a box.

"What's that?" asked Gideon, who had stopped fidgeting now that he had something to look at.

"I don't know," replied Marigold, truthfully.

She was holding a clear plastic box that was only slightly smaller than the briefcase itself. Inside the box she could see several electronic circuit boards, each one crammed from edge to edge with black integrated circuits and colourful components of various shapes and sizes. A mass of delicate cables linked the boards together at multiple points. Marigold also noticed pieces of metal inside that looked like little television aerials. It looked extremely complicated.

"Let me see!" pleaded Gideon, straining to get a better view. But Marigold wasn't going to hand over this treasure just yet.

"Wait, Gideon. Let me have a closer look."

The box appeared to be sealed. Marigold turned it over in her hands but couldn't see any sort of lock, hinge, or anything else that indicated that the box could be opened. All six faces appeared to be completely smooth. Marigold realised that although the box contained lots of complicated electronics, there didn't appear to be any obvious way of working it. Marigold couldn't see any switches or dials anywhere at all. There wasn't even a connector to plug something like a computer keyboard in. After a couple of minutes of further examination, Marigold passed the box over to Gideon. He screwed up his face in concentration as he examined each area in minute detail.

"Aha!" he said triumphantly, after a short while.

"What is it?" queried Marigold.

"Look here. This appears to be where you put the batteries!"

Marigold looked closely at where Gideon was indicating. Just underneath the surface of one of the clear plastic faces was a receptacle that looked as if it could hold some small batteries.

"It looks a bit like the battery compartment of our TV remote control," said Gideon.

Marigold nodded in agreement. "But how do we get the batteries in?" she said.

Gideon started pressing the box at just that spot. Suddenly there was a soft click and a small section of the panel at that point swung open! The two children smiled at each other.

"It's easy when you know how!" said Gideon. He felt very pleased with his discovery.

Marigold examined the opening mechanism in greater detail. It was difficult to work out exactly how it worked because the components were all machined out of the same sort of hard, clear plastic that the box was constructed from. Marigold pressed the small lid down and it shut with another soft click. Marigold examined the area quite closely now, but she still could not see exactly how it worked. Some sort of optical illusion seemed to keep the precise mechanism hidden.

"I'll go and fetch the TV remote control," said Gideon, "and we'll see if the batteries fit." He raced off downstairs.

Marigold held the box in her hands and mulled a few questions over in her mind. What did the box do? Was it a radio or some other communications device? Was it some sort of computer? Was it something that spies or secret agents used? Why were the men in the smart suits and wrap-around sunglasses looking for it? Was this what Dr Black was performing his research on? Marigold was still chewing her bottom lip when Gideon returned with the batteries. She pressed the area over the battery compartment again and the lid dutifully swung up. She carefully inserted the batteries and held her breath.

Soft blue lights, which without power had previously looked like small black components, were now illuminated at various points inside the box. Some twinkled like far-off stars. Some shone brightly and others remained barely lit. The children gazed in wonder at the pretty sight.

"Giddy," said Marigold, without taking her eyes off the box.

"Yes?" replied Gideon, also transfixed by the light display in front of him.

"I have an idea how to find out what this box is for."

THE INSTITUTE

From total darkness, the man patiently and methodically lit seven candles that had been carefully positioned around his study. The contents of his elegantly furnished room were slowly revealed as each candle flickered into life. The antique oak desk was first. Next came the bookcase that lined one wall. The ornate carved fireplace followed. As the man moved around the room performing his solemn task, the richly patterned carpet progressively revealed some colour, and the religious figures in the wall paintings began to look on with interest.

At length, the golden light from all seven candles flickered and danced around the room, teasing the man's shadows as they walked towards the French windows.

The man opened the windows and stood looking out into the warm night air. Far beyond the dim, golden glow of the candles, the low summer moon was throwing a silvery light over the garden. It furnished the grass and the shrubs with an almost frosty glow, at the same time accentuating the man's unnaturally white hair. There was a deadly silence, almost as if the world itself had stopped revolving.

The man waited. Every now and again he would catch a faint honeysuckle fragrance in the air. At these times he would close his eyes and utter a few short words to himself: *'apokalupsis eschaton'*. This cycle continued for some immeasurable time.

A sudden but slight rustling in the shrubbery disturbed his meditations. Without further warning, a dark figure emerged from behind a bush and moved quickly and noiselessly towards him.

"You're late," whispered the man.

"I had trouble getting away this evening," replied the shadowy visitor.

"Never mind. Is it done?"

"Yes. It is done," and the visitor proceeded to hand over a small velvet drawstring bag, which the man took. He stepped back inside his study and moved over to the antique oak desk. Using a key from his pocket he unlocked the centre drawer and placed the bag within. After locking the drawer, he returned to the visitor.

"What about the machine?" he queried.

The visitor hesitated. "I… I… I'm not entirely sure"

"What do you mean you're not entirely sure?" said the man. His voice now had a harder edge to it.

"I can't find it."

The man immediately grabbed the visitor's wrist with a vice-like grip. He gave it a little twist. The visitor bent forward slightly with pain and looked down. Seven small, tattooed stars could just be made out on the back of the man's restraining hand, tracing a curve from his thumb to his little finger.

"What do you mean, you can't find it," hissed the man.

"I've searched everywhere," pleaded the visitor.

"Did he take it home with him?"

"I don't think so… aagh, you're hurting me"

"Have you searched his house?"

"No."

The man let go of the visitor's wrist. "Fool!" he snapped.

"It's not my fault!" pleaded the visitor. "I've done everything that you've asked of me! I said it was too early! The machine isn't even finished!"

The man did not reply. He stood still with his eyes closed for a few minutes. The visitor hardly dared to move, fearful of another violent reaction.

At last, the man spoke. "As you have failed, I will visit the house and recover the machine. You will then complete it."

The visitor gave a shadowy nod. "Whatever you say."

"The Lord is with us. We cannot fail. I will contact you again when I have it."

The visitor slipped silently away with some relief, and the man closed his eyes to continue his meditations on the honeysuckle-filled night.

* * * * * * * *

Marigold and Gideon stood holding their bicycles at the bottom of the long, curved drive that led to the Hermitage Institute.

It was late morning, and the white summer sun was already high in the sky. It had taken the children twenty minutes to cycle across town to the Institute and they were hot.

"Wait for me here, Giddy. I shouldn't be too long," said Marigold cheerfully.

"Are you sure I can't come up with you?" replied Gideon.

"No. It's better if I go alone. I think it will make my plan more believable."

Gideon looked around. He felt decidedly uncomfortable being out in the open next to the main road. There was a small car park and office block on the other side of the road, and it seemed as if there were hundreds of eyes looking at him. Things would only get worse when Marigold disappeared, leaving him holding two bicycles.

"I think I'll hide in these trees," he said, pointing to the thicket that hid the Institute from any prying eyes.

"Good idea," said Marigold. "It's best if you keep out of sight. You'll have some shade as well."

The two children wheeled their bicycles into the mass of trees and leant them against a bush. From here they were sure they couldn't be seen from the main road. Marigold gave Gideon a smile. "I'll be back as quick as I can," she said, and strode off through the trees back towards the drive.

Instead of her usual jeans and a T-shirt, Marigold was wearing a smart, dark green dress. A matching ribbon tamed her hair. She knew that sometimes appearances meant a lot and she wanted to give her plan the best possible chance of success.

The drive curved through the thicket. As Marigold walked it soon gave way to a small car park, beyond which stood the Institute.

In her imagination Marigold had always seen the Institute as some big old building; something like a small manor house with tall imposing pillars either side of a grand front door. She could not have been more wrong. The Institute was a modern square building that seemed to be five storeys of alternating horizontal white plastic and mirrored glass stripes. Marigold made her way to what appeared to be the entrance.

Back in the thicket, Gideon was keeping himself busy by checking the tyre pressures of the two bicycles. On his back he was wearing a small rucksack containing the mysterious box. Marigold had thought it a good idea to bring it along "just in case." Gideon was feeling decidedly jittery after the events of yesterday. He hadn't slept very well at all during the night and had half been expecting someone to knock on the front door. When, at half past three in the morning, his mother had woken him up by accidentally kicking something on her way to the bathroom, he had gripped his sheet so tightly he'd hurt his fingers.

Gideon stood up and looked at the two bicycles. *They're ready if we need to make a quick getaway,*' he told himself, with a certain amount of pride. He was still smiling when a hand from behind gripped his shoulder.

Marigold stood in front of the Institute. The front door was a single piece of mirrored glass with no obvious handle. She tried to push it open, which gave her a funny feeling because it looked as if she was pushing against herself, but the door didn't move. Marigold was in the process of looking around the edges of the glass for a doorbell or an intercom when the glass suddenly slid to one side. Slightly taken aback, she looked in through the entrance and noticed a security guard sitting behind a large wooden console. He beckoned her in.

"Come on in, Miss. What can we do for you?"

Marigold stepped forward into the entrance foyer. It was a large space that seemed to occupy at least three storeys as well as the full width of the building. The only furniture, apart from the security guard's console, was a leather sofa some way off to the left. Marigold felt very insignificant as she made the long walk over to the security guard. This foyer was as big as a church!

"Hello," said Marigold to the guard, in the sweetest voice she could muster. "My name's Marigold Bennett and I am a pupil at St Benedict's School in the town. I have to complete a science project over the summer holidays, and I want to do something unusual. I've heard that the Hermitage Institute gets involved in all sorts of exciting things."

The security guard, who was slouching in his chair, opened his mouth to say something, but Marigold continued talking: "Dr Black works here and he is a neighbour of mine. I wondered if it would be possible to have a word with him. He told me to call in and he would give me some ideas for my project."

Marigold smiled sweetly and for a moment the guard seemed lost for words, but eventually he composed himself.

"Er, I'm not sure that Dr Black is in at the moment, Miss. Was it today that you had an appointment?"

"Oh no, I don't have an appointment," said Marigold. "He just told me to pop in when I was passing. Oh dear, it seems as if I've come all this way for nothing."

The security guard just stared at Marigold and obviously wasn't going to suggest anything, so Marigold went on. "Is there anyone else I can speak to? Perhaps I could speak to Dr Black's assistant?"

"Dr Black doesn't have an assistant, Miss, but I suppose I could give Dr Whitehead a call. Please wait a minute." The security guard picked up a telephone handset from the depths of his console and pressed a button. After a few seconds he spoke into it.

"Dr Whitehead? I've got a young girl in reception by the name of Marigold Bennett. She says that Dr Black was going to advise her about a school project or something, but I know that he's not in the building. She wants to know if there's anybody else she can speak to."

There was a pause whilst the guard listened to the voice at the other end of the telephone. Eventually he replaced the handset and smiled at Marigold.

"Dr Whitehead will be down shortly to see you."

"Thank you," replied Marigold, and she gave him her sweetest smile.

"Take a seat over there, Miss," said the guard, gesturing towards the leather sofa.

Marigold made the long journey over to the sofa and sat down neatly, her hands resting together on her lap. She was already very pleased with herself. Her plan was working! All she had to do now was to be friendly with Dr Whitehead and she was sure she could find out a little more about the mysterious box. She imagined Dr Whitehead looking like some crusty old professor with a mass of white hair and thick white moustache. She thought that he'd be very absent-minded and yet very friendly, telling Marigold all the secrets of the box over a cup of tea.

After a few minutes Marigold heard the soft mechanical whirr of a lift coming to a halt, and a plain looking panel on the wall behind the security guard slid to one side. A woman got out and strode confidently towards the sofa. Marigold thought that she was one of the most elegant women she had ever seen. She was tall, slim and wore an expensive beige suit that somehow seemed to be a perfect fit and have just the right number of buttons. Her hair was a dark blonde colour, with long waves that cascaded artfully over her shoulders. Marigold knew that she was younger than her mother, probably aged about thirty. As the woman drew closer, Marigold thought that her perfect features wouldn't look out of place on the cover of a magazine.

The woman smiled and stretched out her hand as she approached. Marigold stood up to shake it. The woman's delicate perfume preceded her touch by just a moment.

"Hello, I'm Elizabeth Whitehead. You must be Marigold. I understand that you were looking for Dr Black."

Marigold shook Dr Whitehead's hand, and for a moment Marigold felt as if her confidence had gone. All she could concentrate on was the gold bracelets that adorned the doctor's wrist.

"Er, yes I was… I mean I am. I'm writing a school project."

Marigold felt as if this confident, intelligent woman could see right through her. She waited for the Doctor to say something like *"You're lying, and I know why you're really here"* in reply.

But instead the Doctor gave Marigold a winning smile. "We'll have to see what we can do for you then, Marigold. Come with me."

Dr Whitehead turned on her heels and strode back to the lift. Marigold followed a couple of paces behind.

"Hello Clive," said Dr Whitehead to the security guard as she swept by him.

"Hello Doctor," replied Clive with a smile. Marigold noticed that the guard wasn't slouching so much now.

The journey to the top floor only took a few seconds. Marigold knew they were going right to the top because the Doctor had pressed the button with the highest number on the control panel.

As they stepped out of the lift into a corridor, Dr Whitehead struck up the conversation again. "Dr Black is not in the office today, as I'm sure Clive told you. What exactly was it that you were going to talk to him about? You mentioned a school project."

"Yes, Dr Black is a neighbour of mine. He said that he'd tell me a little bit about his work and what goes on at this Institute," said Marigold. She was starting to compose herself and suddenly felt more confident.

"That's strange, because Dr Black never mentioned it to me," said Dr Whitehead. "His work is top secret. He's forbidden to talk about it, or indeed any of the work that we do here at the Institute."

Marigold felt somewhat deflated again, but she knew she had to continue. "Oh," she said. "Perhaps he was just being neighbourly to me. I hope he wasn't humouring me. I thought that he was going to tell me a little about his work. It would be so helpful for my project."

As she spoke, she noticed that they had just passed a door which had Dr Black's name stamped upon it in a bold typeface. *That must be his office,* Marigold thought.

Dr Whitehead opened the very next door along, which had her name stamped upon it in the same fashion.

"Welcome to my office, Marigold. Please, take a seat."

Marigold sat in a plain office chair that was positioned in front of a large grey desk. Dr Whitehead slipped around the back and sat in a somewhat more comfortable brown leather chair. It reclined a little under her weight. Marigold glanced briefly around the room. Behind Dr Whitehead was a long window that ran the full width of the room. From here there was a wonderful view looking back towards the town. Marigold could make out the steeple of St Peter's church in the distance, close to her own home. A small black laptop computer rested on Dr Whitehead's desk. To Marigold's right, simple shelves holding big black cardboard folders adorned the plain white walls. Most of the folders had small, neat writing on their spines. Marigold couldn't read anything from this distance. Set in the wall to the left was a plain white door.

"So, Marigold. Let's talk a little bit about your project and what you might write," said Dr Whitehead. The elegant lady then proceeded to talk about every scientific subject under the sun, or so it seemed to Marigold, except for anything to do with the Institute. Every time that Marigold tried to steer the conversation back to Dr Black, Dr Whitehead would just patiently explain that his work was completely confidential and could not be discussed. Marigold was starting to feel a little downhearted. She realised that if she was going to make any progress, she had to change her plan. Marigold chewed on her bottom lip as her thinking shifted up another gear. Dr Whitehead's voice just seemed to be a droning noise in the background as she eventually realised what she had to do.

"I'm sorry to interrupt you Doctor," said Marigold, "but could I please have a glass of water? I'm very thirsty and I don't feel too well."

"Of course. I'll just go and fetch you one, and please, call me Liz."

"Thanks, Liz."

Dr Whitehead left the office and Marigold sprang into action. She had worked out that the internal white door in Dr Whitehead's office must be a connecting door to Dr Black's office. She tried the door handle and felt relieved when it opened. Marigold darted inside. She knew that she wouldn't have much time.

Dr Black's office was a similar size to Dr Whitehead's, but it felt completely different. Big bookcases covered every inch of available wall space. Colourful spines shouted out strange diverse titles as she glanced around. She noticed one that was concerned with eleven-dimensional space theorems.

Another appeared to be about ancient Haitian voodoo practices. Yet another was about the propagation of microwaves. Marigold felt that the books weren't getting her anywhere, so she turned her attention to the desk. Papers were strewn everywhere. One large open ring binder caught Marigold's eye. She picked it up and read the words on the spine: *'Project WraithTalker.'* Underneath was a small symbol, which looked like an upside-down triangle superimposed over a symmetrical upright cross. Marigold quickly flicked through some of the pages of the folder but all she could find were complicated formulae, and what occasionally appeared to be an electronic circuit diagram. None of it made any sense to Marigold. Feeling somewhat disappointed she returned the folder to the desk and slipped back into Dr Whitehead's office, making sure she closed the connecting door again. She had just sat down when Dr Whitehead reappeared with a glass of water.

"Thanks, Liz," said Marigold as she gulped the water down. Marigold realised that her mouth was completely dry, and the drink was in fact very welcome. "I think I'd better go. Thank you so much for your help and ideas."

"It's been a pleasure, Marigold. I will tell Dr Black that you visited."

Dr Whitehead escorted Marigold to the front of the building and shook her hand again before turning and heading back to the lift. Marigold stepped out down the drive, her head whizzing with numbers, diagrams, and letters. For some reason she couldn't get the words *'Project WraithTalker'* out of her mind. Marigold knew that 'wraith' was another name for a ghost. She also thought that wraiths were unhappy or rather wretched spirits. So, what was, or is, a WraithTalker? Could a WraithTalker be a person? Perhaps it was someone, such as a spiritual medium, who could communicate with ghosts? But if so, then how did this relate to the technical information she'd seen in the ring binder?

At the end of the drive, Marigold stepped back into the thicket. She reached the place where she and Gideon had left their bicycles and stopped in dismay. Not only was there no sign of the bicycles, there was no sign of Gideon! Marigold dashed back to the drive and out onto the road. With her heart racing she quickly looked up and down for any sign of a boy and two bicycles. There was nothing. Marigold started to get very worried. She told herself to remain calm. She knew that she had to think clearly. Perhaps she hadn't checked the right part of the thicket?

Before she could do any more thinking, a crashing noise through the undergrowth at the side of her made her stiffen.

"Gideon!" she exclaimed, as her brother appeared from behind some sort of thick bush.

"Hello Marigold. How did you get on?"

"Never mind that, where have you been!"

"Oh, I've been listening to the radio with Harold."

"What do you mean you've been listening to the radio with Harold?"

"Exactly what I said. He was parked up further down this thicket and he came and surprised me. I nearly jumped out of my skin I can tell you! I decided to wheel our bikes down and join him. I've been drinking his coffee as well, but he's gone now."

Marigold let out a huge sigh of relief. Harold Gilliard was a road sweeper who was known to many of the children of Avonmead. Most adults only saw Harold pushing his small dustcart up and down the town roads, rarely sweeping anything, but most children met him well off the beaten track, in places such as parks and woods and other areas where they played. Harold would push his dustcart to these places "to have a rest" and to listen to his radio and sip from a flask of coffee. Most children loved this likeable fellow. He was someone who talked *with* the children, rather than at them.

"Come on, Giddy, let's fetch our bikes and go. My mind is buzzing with lots of things. I'll tell you about the Institute on the way home."

The two children collected their bicycles and started to pedal.

It was a pity that Marigold had let her mind wander onto other things. It was also a pity that Gideon wasn't concentrating particularly hard at that moment, for if the children had been paying more attention, they would have noticed that a black Mercedes Benz, which had been parked in the car park opposite the Institute, had just started its engine. They would also have noticed that two dark-suited men sitting in the front seats had put on their wrap-around sunglasses.

* * * * * * * *

Mrs Appleby stood in a little side room off the chancel of St Peter's church, softly singing a hymn as she fiddled around inside the cleaner's cupboard. Mrs Appleby was one of those sensible, upright members of the community. She would do anything for anyone. That is why she had stepped in at very short notice to help the vicar when he needed an extra cleaner. That had been eighteen months ago, and she was proud to say that she was still there!

The church of St Peter was a large and beautiful building that, rather unusually, stood right at the edge of Avonmead. Honey-coloured stone had been used for the most part, giving the church a golden and warm appearance.

Inside, the stained-glass windows were one of the church's most beautiful assets and something of a tourist attraction. The ancient arched window at the back of the church, to the west, apparently dated from the sixteenth century.

Certain sections of the church had been part of an older monastery that had once stood on the site. Little of the monastery now remained outside of the church, apart from a few sections of an ancient wall at the far end of the graveyard.

Mrs Appleby spoke aloud as she checked the schedule pinned up inside the cleaning cupboard. "Vacuum the nave; done. Polish the first five pews; done."

"*And was Jerusalem builded here...*" Mrs Appleby started to sing softly to herself as her finger traced the list of tasks down to the bottom. All her chores were complete, except for the one that she enjoyed the most: Check the floral arrangements!

Mrs Appleby adored flowers. Her garden from April through to September was always the envy of the neighbourhood, or so she loved to think. There was nothing she liked better than to pick her surplus flowers, and supplement them with some from the florist to create an arrangement that everyone could appreciate.

Mrs Appleby continued with her hymn as she moved over to fiddle with the flowers that were by the pulpit. "...*among those dark Satanic mills,*" and she pulled out a stem here and replaced a bloom there.

Mrs Appleby was happy, and she probably would have remained cheerful for the rest of the day too if, at that moment, she hadn't accidentally dropped a red carnation onto the floor. As she bent down, she was thinking: '*It must be the cold. It seems to have suddenly gone colder in here today. My hands are freezing!*'

As she arose, she thought she saw something out of the corner of her eye. She turned towards the front pew and suddenly found that she was unable to move a muscle. In less than a second Mrs Appleby felt the blood drain from her body, only to be replaced with icy water. The hairs on the back of her head prickled as if they were rising. Sitting in the front pew, only a few short feet away, was a middle-aged man. It wasn't so much that it was a man in front of her. It wasn't even the fact that he was dressed in some sort of crimson robes that made him look like a monk. It wasn't even the fact that he was grinning at her. It was the fact that she could see right through him!

Mrs Appleby dropped the carnation once more and screamed.

THE CHURCH

After fifteen minutes of cycling the children were close to their home at the northern edge of town. Marigold had related her experiences at the Institute to an eager Gideon.

"They obviously don't know at the Institute that Dr Black is dead," reasoned Gideon, shouting over his shoulder as he cycled. The children were riding in single file down a fragrant lane, which had open fields to the right behind a hedgerow, and a row of neat little cottages to the left.

"No," replied Marigold. "In fact, I wonder if anyone else apart from us and the men in dark suits DO know. It could be that Dr Black's still lying there. He probably is if the men haven't reported his death."

Marigold shivered a little as she said this. Even though she hadn't known Dr Black, Marigold didn't like to think of his body lying unclaimed in the house. She somehow felt as if he might be lonely, even though she knew that was silly.

"Don't forget that his murderer, if he *was* murdered, also knows that he's there," pointed out Gideon

"Possibly," said Marigold, and she started to chew on her bottom lip. She wondered if she ought to return to the house and find out if Dr Black really *was* still there. If so, maybe she could tip the police off anonymously.

The children cycled along in silence. Marigold had a feeling that there was something obvious she was missing, but she couldn't quite put her finger on it.

After a while Gideon sighed. "Phew, we really must remember to bring drinks with us." He was feeling decidedly hot and sweaty now after cycling along in the full sun.

Marigold didn't reply. At that moment she was remembering the mistake she had almost made yesterday, when she had not properly checked to see if the men in dark suits had been following them. It had given both children a terrible fright when her mother had unexpectedly rang the doorbell.

"Stop here a minute, Giddy," she called out.

Gideon dutifully applied his brakes and put one foot down to steady himself. He was just turning round to see what Marigold wanted when she cautioned him. "No, don't turn around just yet. I want to check something."

Marigold carefully turned her head and squinted back up the lane. She didn't expect to see anything, so it was a bit of a shock to find that she could just about make out a black car in the distance. She squinted harder. The car appeared to be moving, albeit very slowly, and then it stopped. Although it was only a tiny image, Marigold was sure the car was a Mercedes Benz.

"Giddy, I think we're being followed by the men in dark suits and sunglasses."

Gideon gave a little squeak as he comprehended what Marigold had just said. "Let's make a run for it!" he urged, standing on one of his pedals as if to race off.

Marigold was swift in her reply: "No. Listen to me carefully," she said. Her mind had already raced around the possibilities. "We're going to carry on cycling as normal for a while."

Gideon didn't look happy at this suggestion. "Let's ring the doorbell of one of these houses and ask for help," he pleaded, looking over at the row of neat little cottages to the left.

"No," said Marigold. "For one thing the owner might not be in, for another we might be endangering somebody who's innocent, and finally the men will probably just wait for us to come out again. We'll be forced into calling the police, and I don't think we want to do that just yet."

Gideon was amazed at his sister's quick thinking, but he was still very worried. "So how does cycling on as normal help?" he asked.

"It seems to me that the men are just following us. They don't want to create a scene by confronting us on these roads. My guess is that they're trying to find out where we live."

Gideon felt chilled as he contemplated the men in dark suits finally finding out where they lived.

Marigold continued swiftly with her instructions. "In about three hundred metres there's a little footpath off over the open fields to the right. Do you remember it? It's another way over to Blackthorn Pond."

Gideon nodded.

"When we reach it, we must get our bikes over the stile and cycle away as fast as we can along the path. The car won't be able to follow us, and we'll be much too fast on our bikes for anyone on foot."

Gideon started to feel a little better. "We could cut across to Carter Lane and make our way back from there," he suggested.

"That's exactly what we're NOT going to do," said Marigold, "but I'll explain more shortly. For now, let's make our escape."

The children started to pedal again.

"Not too fast," cautioned Marigold. "Let's go at our normal speed. We don't want the men to get suspicious." She was sure that the car would be rolling after them again, but she didn't dare to look back.

It took the children a couple of minutes to reach the stile. It seemed like a lifetime to Gideon. At any moment he expected the car to race past and cut them off and he listened carefully for any sound of an engine behind them.

Marigold gave some more instructions as they slid to a halt: "Giddy, climb over. I'll pass the bikes to you."

Gideon did as he was told but it wasn't long before Marigold realised that she'd made a mistake. She wasn't strong enough to lift even one bike up as high as the top bar of the stile. As she struggled, Gideon clambered back to help. The children could now hear the roar of a car behind them. Gideon looked up to see the black Mercedes racing down the lane. "Quick!" he shouted.

The two children working together managed somehow to manhandle both bikes over the wooden structure. They clambered over themselves just as the black Mercedes skidded to a halt, metres away. The children were on their bikes in a flash. Marigold was first away, with Gideon slightly behind. He'd found that his legs were a bit wobbly at first and wouldn't connect properly with the pedals.

"HEY YOU TWO! COME BACK HERE!" barked a man with a deep booming voice. Marigold risked a quick look over her shoulder to see someone in a dark suit and wrap-around sunglasses dashing to the stile.

The two children pedalled furiously across the field and didn't stop until one minute later, when the footpath reached the brow of a hill. They looked back to see the man still standing at the stile. He had obviously decided, as Marigold had predicted, that it wasn't worth chasing the children on foot. The driver was still in the car.

"I think that the man who's standing at the stile is checking to see in which direction we're heading," said Marigold, somewhat out of breath. "He's trying to keep us in sight for as long as possible. The man in the car is probably inspecting a map. My guess is that they'll try to work out which road we're heading for and try to intercept us. Let's head north, as if we're making for Carter Lane. As soon as we're out of sight we'll cut to the west and make for St Peter's church. The churchyard backs onto the fields and we can slip in unnoticed through the back-wall gate. We can then hide in the churchyard until we think it's safe to head home. The men will never guess where we are. They'll be too busy searching the roads."

Gideon though that this was an excellent plan. "Let's go!" he said, and pedalled off.

* * * * * * * *

The large, windowless room was panelled on all four sides with expensive oak. A rich blue carpet covered the floor. The only furniture present was a highly polished brass bed, which had been carefully positioned under a large and elaborate crystal chandelier. A pure white blanket lay draped over the bed, long enough to touch the floor on three sides.

An old man lay under the blanket, his shrivelled head resting lightly on a clean and crisp pillow. White, wispy strands of his hair lay spread out over the pillow like ghostly threads of light from a pale and dying sun.

The old man watched as two children, a boy and a girl, cycled away across a field.

"The children are getting away," said a disembodied voice.

The old man wet his lips with a few soft licks. "Closer, closer," he hissed, and one corner of his mouth twitched as he immediately had the sensation of travelling across the field at high speed. It wasn't long before he felt quite close to the children, but they continued to pedal furiously away, seemingly oblivious to the presence that was now tracking them.

The children reached the brow of a small hill, but instead of continuing onwards they skidded to a halt and turned sharply around. The old man immediately had the sensation of coming to a dead stop a few metres away. The boy looked defiant and ready to fight. The girl, however, appeared to be tired and worried. The smart green dress she was wearing was crinkled and dusty. She was breathing hard, and it was a few moments before she managed to compose herself and mouth a few silent words to the boy.

The old man looked at the children, licking his lips with a trembling tongue.

"What shall we do?" asked the disembodied voice.

"I want those children," rasped the old man. "Bring them to me NOW!"

* * * * * * * *

The picturesque honey-coloured church of St Peter sat a little to one side of the churchyard. The two children wheeled their bikes through the rear gate, and followed a narrow path that weaved its way through some rather large tombstones towards the outside back wall of the church. Some of the ancient monuments were decorated with little stone angels. Gideon found them a little disconcerting and he was glad that the sun was still shining brilliantly. He thought that it would be a scary place to be after dark, although he didn't share his thoughts with his sister; he knew that she would chide him.

The gravestones closest to the church were the oldest. They were of various sizes and colours, ranging from a deep grey to a light mossy green. The wording on most had been weathered away and almost none of them stood perfectly upright. They looked like broken teeth, mused Gideon.

Marigold had deliberately led them to an area at the back of the church. "Let's find a peaceful place in the shade," she said.

It only took the children a minute to find a pleasant grassy spot, shielded from general view of the rest of the churchyard by two large headstones. To the rear, an ancient broken wall gave cover from anybody who might be following from across the fields.

The children leant their bicycles against a large headstone and Gideon slipped off the rucksack containing the mysterious box. He flopped down on the grass with some relief, looking up at the sky.

"This is too much excitement for me," he said, glancing over towards Marigold. She smiled back at him, thinking that he didn't really mean it.

"At least I'm sure of one thing now," she said.

"What's that?"

"Those men are not from the police. Police officers do not go around following children at a distance. They don't have to. They do things like arrest people and take them in for questioning."

Gideon didn't feel any happier for hearing this. "So, who are these men, and what do they want with us?"

"I can't even begin to suspect who the men are, but I know that they're after this box." Marigold reached over and dragged the rucksack towards her. She opened it up and slid the mysterious box out. "The fact that they've been chasing us again today proves it. They obviously didn't find what they were looking for in Dr Black's house."

Gideon was frowning. "So that means that they probably won't give up."

"Not if it means a lot to them," replied Marigold, grimly. She looked thoughtful as she turned the box over and over a few times in her hands.

"I'm going to see if I can deduce anything about this," she said. "I remember Sherlock Holmes finding out a lot about someone who had written a letter, just by looking at the envelope. Even the way the stamp was stuck on told him something."

"Well, there are no stamps on this box," said Gideon.

"I know there aren't, silly, but we might be able to find out something."

Marigold started with the electronic circuit boards. There were seven in total, mostly of different sizes. She didn't understand what the components mounted on them were at all. Some had letters and numbers printed on them. Others were just plain. She wished that she knew something about electronics, or even knew someone who did. She remembered the circuit drawings in the folder on Dr Black's desk. He had obviously been some sort of expert.

Marigold then started to look at one of the boards itself, rather than the components. It was green in colour and seemed to have little tracks on it running this way and that, connecting various components together. Marigold's eyes continued to wander until they eventually widened when she noticed a little symbol etched into the corner of the board. It was a little cross with an upside-down triangle on it!

"Project WraithTalker!" she exclaimed.

Gideon, who had been resting with his eyes closed, sat up at once. "What did you say?"

"Look. Here, on the corner of this board. It's the same symbol that was on a ring binder I found in Dr Black's study. I think that this box is something to do with project WraithTalker!"

"WraithTalker?" asked Gideon, quizzically. "What sort of weird word is that?"

"I don't know," admitted Marigold. "A wraith is a sort of ghost or restless spirit, I think."

"Surely this can't be a machine for talking to ghosts?" queried Gideon. "There's no such thing as ghosts."

Marigold looked thoughtful. "Perhaps wraith is a codename for something," she said. "Maybe it's a special name for 'secret agent' and this is a machine for talking to secret agents?"

Gideon nodded. This seemed entirely plausible to him. "They used code breaker machines in the Second World War," he said. "Perhaps this is a high-tech version? Maybe those men in dark suits and sunglasses are from a foreign power and they're anxious to get hold of our codes?"

Marigold looked thoughtful. Sherlock Holmes would only make deductions based on hard facts. It was all too easy to speculate and be led down a false trail. She knew that she still had to keep an open mind.

Marigold took the box back from Gideon and turned her attention to the small pieces of metal that looked like small television aerials. There were six of them in total. Each one seemed to be made from some sort of greyish purple metal that she hadn't seen before. Marigold couldn't even put a name to the colour. Each one had a little black wire running from it to a circuit board, and it didn't take her long to realise that each aerial was pointing outwards from a different face of the box. Did this ensure that a signal could be picked up from any direction?

Marigold was starting to struggle now. Looking for clues with something as complicated and strange as this box was not easy. She turned it over repeatedly in her hands, looking for inspiration.

"I do wish we'd brought a drink and some chocolate with us," said Gideon lazily, who by now was lying down again with his eyes closed.

Marigold ignored him and started to chew her bottom lip. She was determined to find out *something* more about this box.

She studied the black battery holder. The little wire leading from it was tightly coiled like an old-fashioned telephone handset cord. Marigold's thoughts turned back to the wire she had seen yesterday, stretching down from the table to Dr Black's body in the blankets. Of course! Coiled wires were usually only attached to something that could be moved, to keep the connections neat but flexible. Could the battery holder itself be removed from the compartment? Marigold swiftly pressed the area over the battery compartment and the cover opened with a soft click. Marigold's little fingers reached inside and tried to pull the holder out. It wouldn't move. Using a combination of sight and touch she felt all around it; there seemed to be a little button at the opposite end to the coiled cord. She pressed the button and to her great delight the battery holder slid to one side! Six little numbered dials peered out from underneath. Each was set to zero, although Marigold noticed that each one could be set to any number up to nine.

"Giddy!"

"Uh," moaned Gideon, half asleep.

"Look!"

Gideon sat up with his eyes barely open. The fact that he hadn't had much rest last night was obviously catching up with him.

"What is it?" he yawned.

Marigold showed him the open compartment and pointed out the numbered dials. Gideon started to perk up.

"Let's put the batteries back in and we'll see what happens when I change the settings. They're all at zero now, so we can easily leave the machine as it was if we have to."

Gideon fumbled in one of the many outer pockets of his rucksack and produced two small batteries. He handed them to Marigold who slid the holder back into place before inserting them. She then slid the holder out of the way again to reveal the dials.

The box twinkled into life, but in open daylight it was harder to see the little blue lights.

"Let's sit further into the shadow of this gravestone," said Marigold. "We'll be able to see the colours a bit better."

The children shuffled along until they were leaning against the back of one of the rather large headstones that had been shielding them from general view. They had the box resting on the grass between them. In the dark shadow cast by the stone it was easier to make out the beautiful blue twinkling.

"Right, I'm going to turn one of these dials *here*," and as she said it Marigold turned the first dial to number one. Almost immediately the pattern of flashing lights within the box changed. Lights that had previously been off suddenly started to flash. Others that had been dim appeared to glow brighter. Others that had been slowly flickering seemed to speed up.

Marigold tried different settings. Every time she changed one of the dials by as much as a single number, the pattern of the flashing lights seemed to change completely.

"I know," said Gideon, "let's dial in our telephone number."

Marigold gave Gideon one of her looks, but he wasn't watching, preferring instead to keep his eyes on the mesmerising display. Marigold decided not to waste time arguing with him, so she set the dials as requested: five, five, five, eight, one and nine. Secretly she was somewhat intrigued herself to find out what the pattern of lights would be. The children weren't disappointed. There seemed to be a certain rhythm to the light display now.

"It's almost musical," said Gideon, struggling to find words to describe the way that the lights flashed and blinked.

Marigold agreed, and the two children sat for a couple of minutes, completely hypnotised. Gideon shivered a little but put it down to the fact that they were now sitting in the shade.

Without warning, a muffled scream from behind shook the children out of their daydream. They looked at each other and before either of them could say anything, the scream came again, and then it came once more.

"Where did *that* come from?" said Gideon, looking like a frightened rabbit.

"The church, I think," replied Marigold, getting to her feet.

"Not again! I think we better leave well alone this time," said Gideon hopefully, but as usual he knew what the answer was going to be.

"It sounded like a woman. Put the box back into your bag. We'll have to go and see what's happened."

Gideon slid the battery holder back into place and removed the batteries. He groaned a little as he put the box back into the rucksack. He decided that all this excitement was getting too much for him after all. He could already envisage another dead body, this time in the church!

"Look!" shouted Marigold, pointing.

Gideon stared over to where Marigold was indicating. On the other side of the churchyard, beyond the front porch of the church, an elderly woman was running as fast as she could down the path towards the road.

"I think it's Mrs Appleby," said Marigold, squinting.

Mrs Appleby was well known to the children. She lived just around the corner from their house.

"Do you think she's just killed someone?" said Gideon quietly.

"Don't be stupid, Giddy. Mrs Appleby wouldn't hurt a fly. No, I think she's the one who's just called out. Something's frightened her!"

"It could be a mouse," suggested Gideon, desperately trying to damp down the adrenalin fire that he knew was rising in his sister.

"We'd better go and find out," and with that Marigold jumped up and jogged off around the tombstones at the side of the church.

Gideon slipped the rucksack onto his back and had a distinct feeling of déjà vu as he trotted off after his sister.

In the entrance porch of the church the children stopped and stared. The heavy oak door had been left wide open. Mrs Appleby had obviously been in a terrible hurry. The children listened for a while, half afraid to enter. A gentle musty breeze flowed into their faces from within.

"I wonder what frightened her?" said Marigold, suddenly thinking that perhaps someone had tried to attack poor Mrs Appleby.

Gideon didn't reply. His eyes were scanning the parts of the floor he could see for the subtle movements of a mouse or a rat.

"We'd better go in and have a look around," said Marigold, and she stepped cautiously through the doorway.

In entering the church, she had the same sense of space that she'd had when entering the Hermitage Institute. Gideon followed, rather nervously. He found the stale air rather oppressive. It seemed to be a mixture of damp stonework and old furniture polish.

"Can we go now?" he whispered.

"No, not until we've had a look around."

It all seemed deadly quiet as the children slowly walked down the centre aisle. Dark, regimented wooden pews filled the spaces to both sides. The light that streamed through the stained-glass window behind them cast thousands of colourful dots around their feet. They walked steadily towards the gloom at the front, looking left and right as they checked each pew. Saints from the smaller stained-glass windows along each wall seemed to smile kindly down upon the pair as they slowly crept forward.

At the lectern near the head of the pews, Marigold stopped and looked back. Nothing could be seen or heard, although her gaze was inevitably drawn to the stunning colours and patterns of the ancient stained-glass window above the rear door. Gideon picked up a red carnation from the floor.

"It all seems very quiet," said Marigold. Gideon gave a nod in reply, hardly daring to break the silence.

"Let's have a look up here," she whispered, pointing up towards the chancel. Gideon glanced to where Marigold was indicating, and he swallowed quite audibly.

The air was distinctly cooler as the children left the nave and softly stepped towards the altar. Gideon felt almost claustrophobic. The walls and the wooden choir stalls seemed to somehow press against him. The children reverently approached the altar and Gideon had a strange urge to kneel as he got close. Even Marigold felt herself giving a little bow. As she did so, a voice behind them cut through the air like thunder.

"Can I help you?"

Both children jumped and Gideon gave a little yelp. He felt his hands tingle and his knees go weak. Unable to move, it was Marigold at his side who was the first to react. She swung herself around, fully prepared to fight. The man now standing in front of her, however, made her stop and stare. He must certainly have been well over two metres tall.

"I'm sorry, children. I didn't mean to startle you."

By now Gideon had also managed to turn around. His mouth opened and closed like a dying fish as he looked at the giant before him. Marigold's eyes swiftly scanned the handsome man's face, trying to read his intentions. She soon relaxed. He looked calm and kind. He appeared to be about thirty-five, although it was difficult to tell. His hair was completely white, and Marigold thought that perhaps he had dyed it that colour because somehow it didn't look natural. The man was standing in the gloom, yet his eyes seemed to twinkle with little fires as he looked down on the children.

"I'm the vicar here. The Reverend Charles Orle."

"I'm Marigold and this is my brother Gideon," said Marigold, with some relief.

The vicar smiled down at Gideon. "That's a good Biblical name."

Gideon smiled weakly back, not sure whether he had to say anything in reply.

"We heard someone screaming and came to investigate," said Marigold.

"So did I," said the vicar. "I had the windows of the vicarage wide open in this heat. I was concerned because I knew Mrs Appleby was cleaning in here."

"We saw her running away as fast as she could," blurted out Gideon.

"Oh, I see," said the vicar with a slight frown. "I hope it wasn't anything serious. Perhaps she saw a mouse."

Gideon glanced over at Marigold with a slightly triumphant look on his face, but Marigold didn't look back.

"I was concerned in case someone else had been in here," she said.

"Well, there was nobody in the side room which I came through," said the vicar, "and I suppose that you two have walked through the nave?"

Marigold and Gideon nodded.

"I therefore think it's safe to say that there's nobody else involved," continued the vicar. "All the other doors should be locked. I'll have a quick look around myself and then phone Mrs Appleby to see what the matter is."

The vicar fixed his gaze on Gideon. "May I ask why you're carrying that carnation?"

Gideon glanced down at the red flower he had picked up a moment ago.

"Er, I found it on the floor," he said, reddening a little with embarrassment. He held it out and the vicar took it, but not before both Marigold and Gideon had noticed the neat little line of seven stars tattooed on the back of his hand, tracing a curve from his thumb to his little finger.

GHOSTS

Marigold took a sip of coffee and handed the plastic cup back to Harold.

"Thanks," she said, gratefully.

"No problem," said Harold, smiling. He offered the cup to Gideon, who gently refused it by putting his hand up.

"So, what did you want to ask me?" asked the road sweeper, cheerily.

Harold was a tall, lean man in his early fifties. Flat, thinning dark hair somehow seemed to lie sideways across his head. Ripe chestnut brown eyes stood out from a sallow face, and a rather large and dimply nose was perched above a thin and rather cruel-looking mouth. Gideon had often thought that his mouth seemed completely out of keeping with his character. Harold usually wore an old smelly grey raincoat and brown trousers. Today was no exception. He hardly ever wore his fluorescent safety jacket. "It makes me stand out," he had once said to Gideon.

The two children had found Harold in one of his favourite haunts: a quiet bench next to a small pool in one of the town parks. It was shielded from general view by a few small silver-barked trees. Harold's dustcart had been pushed under one of them. His radio was sitting on the bench next to him and a quiet song drifted from it. The children could only just make out the tune. Anybody passing along the path on the other side of the trees would have heard nothing.

"Harold, what do you know about the Hermitage Institute?" asked Marigold.

Harold squinted and looked out over the water as he sipped his coffee.

"Very little," he replied. "The work there seems to be very hush-hush. I honestly can't tell you much. Because of the secrecy I used to think that they carried out work for the Government, but from what I've heard it's actually a privately funded institute carrying out research into tropical diseases or something like that."

Marigold looked disappointed. She and Gideon had deliberately sought out Harold that morning in the hope that he would be able to tell them something about the Institute. Harold was one of the big players in Avonmead's gossip machine. A snippet of news picked up in one part of town could be transmitted to another just as soon as he had wheeled his cart there. It was something of a disappointment to hear him say that the Institute didn't appear to carry out secret projects for the Government. Gideon had rather favoured the WraithTalker being used as a secret communications device for spies. What possible connection could it have to tropical diseases?

"Has this got something to do with your visit there yesterday?" continued Harold.

"Sort of," Marigold nodded.

Even though she regarded Harold as a friend, she didn't want to tell him too much. She knew that anything of interest she said to him could be passed on to someone else at an adult level. She still didn't feel the time was right just yet.

Marigold stared out over the sparkling water. She hardly noticed the pair of ducks that were slowly making their way together across the surface.

It wasn't long before the road sweeper broke the silence again. "I was surprised to find young Gideon in the thicket yesterday. Mind you, I think he was more surprised to see me!"

Harold chuckled, and his eyes twinkled as he glanced over towards Gideon, who gave a rather embarrassed smile back. "What were you doing up there anyway? Gideon said that it was something for school."

"Yes, I was looking for ideas for a science project, but I think I've chosen something now," said Marigold, feeling rather uncomfortable in lying to Harold.

"What is it?" queried the road sweeper, speaking into his cup but keeping his gaze fixed on Marigold.

"Oh, I've decided to write a piece about ghosts," said Marigold casually, saying the first thing that came into her head.

Harold spluttered into his coffee cup. "Ghosts? What makes you interested in ghosts?"

"It seems like an interesting subject, that's all," said Marigold nonchalantly.

Harold kept his eyes on Marigold. "You ought to go and see Mrs Appleby then."

Gideon gave a sort of snort and even Marigold's jaw visibly dropped.

"What did you say?" she said.

"I said that you ought to have a word with Mrs Appleby. She saw a ghost in St Peter's church yesterday."

Marigold and Gideon looked at each other in stunned silence. Mrs Appleby had seen a ghost in the church? Perhaps that was the reason why the poor woman had gone running from the building! Gideon's eyes widened as he thought back to the previous day. He and Marigold had been in the church immediately after Mrs Appleby. They might have been in there with a ghost!

Marigold looked excited. Gideon could see that she was bursting to tell him something but was obviously holding her tongue because of Harold. Harold himself looked pleased that he'd found a snippet of news that had surprised the children.

"Oh yes, I heard that she'd seen the Red Monk again."

"The Red Monk?" Gideon looked astonished.

"He's been seen before, though I think it must be close to seventy years ago when he last appeared," said Harold, looking thoughtful. "At least to my knowledge. I remember my old Dad telling me about him when I was a nipper."

"Why is he called the Red Monk?" asked Gideon, suddenly getting a bit nervous and imagining a woeful looking soul with blood dripping from his hands and head.

"It's to do with the robes he wears. They're red in colour although he's dressed like a proper monk. When my old Dad, God rest his soul, told me about him, he said that he'd been spotted about thirty years previous by the new vicar of the Parish. The vicar hadn't seen the monk's face, because he'd got his red hood up, but he was apparently kneeling in some sort of silent prayer in the vestry. It gave the vicar the shivers, I can tell you. Apparently it got too much for him and he left soon afterwards."

"Did Mrs Appleby see the monk kneeling?" asked Gideon.

"No, he was sitting in the front pew, just looking at her. Smiling he was, by all accounts. Proper shook her up it did. One minute the pew's all empty and the next there's a Red Monk gawping at her."

Marigold looked more composed now. "Did she say what he looked like?"

"Oh, I dunno about that," said Harold. "The way I heard it she just saw this fellow in the front pew and ran off, screaming."

"Well, that's certainly something for my school project. Do you believe that she really did see a ghost, Harold?"

Harold pondered for a while before replying. "Yup. I reckon that there are a few who can. Mrs Appleby must have the power."

Marigold looked thoughtful. Gideon noticed that she had begun to chew her bottom lip again. He thought that he would have been petrified if a Red Monk had materialised whilst he and Marigold had been in the church. It was bad enough that the Reverend Orle had suddenly appeared and given them both a fright. That was an interesting point, he thought. Had the Reverend Orle seen anything after they had left? Marigold must have been thinking along the same lines.

"St Peter's has got a new vicar, hasn't it?" she asked. "Did he see anything?"

"Haven't heard anything," said Harold. "Mind you," he continued, leaning forward and lowering his voice as if someone might be listening, "he's a strange one he is."

"Why's that?" whispered back Marigold, moving closer.

"Well, he turns up out of nowhere after old Sam Moreton retired. He's allegedly spent much of his life abroad, doing missionary work. Africa mostly. The story goes that he had to be brought back because of certain troubles."

Gideon, who had been straining to hear what was being said, looked puzzled. "What do you mean, 'certain troubles'?" he asked.

"Well," and at this point Harold sat briefly upright again and looked around to check that nobody was in earshot, "they say that he started dabbling with things that he ought not to have dabbled with."

"I wonder what that was?" pondered Marigold aloud.

"I dunno, but the way I heard it his faith was severely tested."

Harold sat up, and the two children shuffled into more comfortable positions on the bench.

"The ladies like him though. Attendances at church have been up since he's been on the scene. Oh yes, I've spoken to many a woman who's got her eye on the Reverend Orle."

"He's a single man then?" smiled Marigold.

"Yup. Lives in that big old vicarage by himself. He'd be quite a catch I reckon," twinkled back Harold.

Marigold looked back over the pool. Specks of sunlight reflected off the surface, exploding like miniature short-lived stars. The patterns reminded Marigold a little of the twinkling blue lights of the WraithTalker. Marigold was beginning to formulate another action plan and was anxious to explain it to

Gideon, but before that she had another question for the road sweeper.

"Harold," she began.

"Mmm," replied Harold, his mouth back in his coffee cup.

"What do you think ghosts are?"

Marigold knew that Harold's general knowledge was astonishing. It was something she attributed to his listening to the radio all day. On more than one occasion he had successfully helped the children with their homework when every other source of reference had failed.

Harold licked his lips before answering. "Nobody knows what ghosts are, or even if they exist you might say, but I reckon that there's too much smoke around for there not to be any fire. I think that, if you disregard the deluded, the charlatans and the fame seekers, ghosts seem to be unfortunate souls who haunt the place of their death. It's almost as if they died unjustly, or perhaps died leaving some unfinished business. There seems to be something that keeps their spirit here on Earth. It stops them from getting to where they ought to be."

Harold looked out over the water again and the two children followed his gaze.

"Most people seem to be frightened of ghosts, but I've never heard of a ghost doing anybody any harm. If anything, I feel sorry for them."

After a couple of moments Marigold stood up. "Thanks Harold. We've got to be going. See you around."

"Bye Harold," added Gideon, taking his cue from his sister.

Harold smiled weakly back, and unless Marigold was much mistaken there was moisture in his eyes.

Marigold and Gideon sat on the back patio of their house, eating their evening meal. The early evening sun was just starting to lose its strength, bathing everything in a yellowy-orange light.

Ruth Bennett's head popped out through the open back door. "Does anyone want any more salad?"

"No thanks Mum," said the children, almost in unison. Their mother's head disappeared, and Gideon turned to Marigold.

"Tell me again what you've been thinking."

Marigold finished chewing on a piece of chicken before answering. "I've been thinking back to the churchyard. It's just too much of a coincidence. You know it is. We're using a machine that's called a WraithTalker outside a church at the precise moment that the Red Monk appears to Mrs Appleby. What does that tell you?"

"I know what it's telling me. I'm just too scared to believe it!"

"Giddy, we'd better start believing it. The thing that really scares me is that we might be like toddlers playing with matches. Who knows what we're doing by operating the WraithTalker? We just don't understand it. Every time we switch it on we could be conjuring up all sorts of spirits. We're dabbling with something that could be incredibly dangerous."

Gideon looked worried. The furrowed lines on his forehead twitched a little as he thought. "It might be that the only person who did understand it was Dr Black, and now he's dead," he said. "I think those men in dark suits know what it is. They understand its importance. That's why they're so keen to get hold of it. I really don't think that they'll stop at anything."

"Giddy, I have to tell you something…"

But before Marigold could continue, her mother came out holding a tray with three bowls on it. "It's ice-cream for dessert. Is that OK?"

Both children nodded. Gideon wanted to hear what Marigold had to say, but he knew he had to be patient.

"What did you two get up to today?"

"We chatted to Harold for a bit," started Gideon, but he quickly fell silent when Marigold caught his eye.

"You know I don't like you talking to that man," said his mother. "He gives me the creeps."

"He's alright Mum," said Marigold, "really."

"That's as maybe, but I don't want you hanging around him for too long, OK?"

Both children nodded and Marigold decided to change the subject. "Mum, do you believe in ghosts?"

Her mother took a mouthful of ice-cream and shook her head. "Nwop," she said, quickly swallowing. "Never seen one and I don't know anybody who has. I reckon people dream them up. Most of them are seen by people snoozing in their bed."

Marigold thought about Mrs Appleby. She hadn't been in her bed when she saw the Red Monk, unless she'd taken a rest from her cleaning and had taken a nap. Marigold doubted that. "Have you heard about any local ghosts?" she persisted.

"No, I don't think I have," said her mother thoughtfully. "There was a story of one that used to haunt Kites Farm. You know the place, near to where your grandmother used to live. It was said that the ghost of a maid haunted the place, back from the time when the farm was a country house. The legend goes that the maid killed her mistress and was subsequently hanged for her crime. Lots of old places have stories about resident ghosts. They're just interesting stories, that's all. Now eat up your ice-cream before it melts."

The children finished their dessert and Mrs Bennett took the bowls back into the house. Gideon waited until he was sure that his mother wasn't coming out again and then he leaned over towards Marigold. "What were you going to tell me?" he whispered.

Marigold broke off from chewing her bottom lip to look at her brother. "Well, firstly you know that I'm worried that we're dabbling with something that we don't understand and could be dangerous. Then, even without the frightening prospect of ghosts popping up all over the place, we've got the men in dark suits and sunglasses chasing us. I'm really worried about that. I don't think they're going to give up and I don't know what they'll do to us if they catch us. I think that we have no choice but to tell Mum and the police everything that we know."

Marigold went back to chewing her lip. Gideon didn't know whether to feel relieved or worried. For the most part he just wanted the adventure of the past few days to end. He desperately wanted the responsibility passed onto someone else. But he was also worried that the two children were going to get into an awful lot of trouble, especially for not reporting Dr Black's death. Gideon thought again about the recent events: the finding of the WraithTalker, being chased by the men in dark suits twice, the mystery of the Hermitage Institute and, biggest of all, the reappearance of a local ghost who hasn't been seen for seventy years. He felt some butterflies taking flight in his stomach. There was a brief instant where he suspected he was enjoying himself, but he quickly managed to stifle it.

Marigold turned towards him. "Giddy, there are a few things that I've got to do before we tell our story to anyone."

Gideon's butterflies intensified their dance. He was now suddenly very sure that he wanted the adventure to end right here and now.

"Don't look so worried," continued Marigold. "It doesn't involve you."

Gideon expected to feel relieved, but he sensed that his sister was going to be in danger. He felt his heart give a little jump, almost as if it was leaping to her defence. "What are you going to do?"

"I'm going back to Dr Black's house. Tonight. I've got to check three things. Firstly, I've got to see if that poor man is still lying on the floor. I still feel guilty about leaving him. He deserves more respect. The second thing is that I'm sure there will be some information concerning the WraithTalker in his house and I just *have* to find out more about it. My curiosity is getting the better of me. If we let the authorities look after things now, I don't think we'll ever hear about the machine again. Last, and perhaps most of all, I've finally realised what it is about the doctor's telephone that's been bugging me. I've got to try something."

Gideon's mouth must have been open because his smiling sister reached across and gently lifted his chin up.

At precisely midnight Marigold silenced her little alarm clock and swung her legs sleepily around and out of bed. It took her a few seconds to stand up because the warm softness of her quilt was longing to have her back in its folds. She hadn't realised that she was going to feel so sleepy. Concentrating on the mission ahead she quickly got dressed and picked up Gideon's rucksack. The heavy feel of it reassured her tired mind that the WraithTalker was still inside. She also mentally checked off the few extra items she'd packed: a torch, because she didn't want to turn any lights on at Dr Black's house, and a small pencil and pad in case she needed to jot down any information she might find out about the WraithTalker.

Marigold stepped onto the landing and listened. From within her mother's bedroom she could hear regular deep breathing. Good! Her mother was fast asleep. There was no noise from Gideon's room. He must also be out for the count. Marigold clutched the rucksack to her chest and slipped silently downstairs. Already her thoughts were with the coming adventure. What would she find? If Dr Black's body was still there it would be a little scary, but a dead person couldn't hurt you. Marigold suddenly thought about the Red Monk. Was he dead or was he real? Could he hurt anyone? She was still thinking about this as she reached the hall and came to an abrupt stop. A big black shadow was blocking the front door! Her heart skipped a beat before she realised it was Gideon. He must have been waiting for her and had fallen asleep on the mat. Marigold couldn't leave the house that way without waking him. She wondered if perhaps he had got something to tell her. She reasoned that he would have already woken her if it had been important. Did he want to come with her? She had been rather firm with him in insisting that she went out by herself. Then Marigold noticed that he was still in his pyjamas. She realised that all he probably wanted to do was to wish her good luck. She wanted to bend down and kiss the sleeping figure, but she was scared it would wake him, so she turned and sneaked away, leaving by the back door out into the cool night air.

It didn't take Marigold long to reach Dr Black's house. She'd walked briskly down the suburban streets and not a single car had passed her by. It had seemed strange at first to be out alone whilst most other people were sleeping, but it was a feeling she quickly got used to.

She was now standing near the house, right next to the small wall that she and Gideon had hopped across two days ago. The house was away from most streetlamps, and it appeared to be cloaked in a deep, dark veil. There had been light from the moon when Marigold had begun her short journey, but now thick clouds all but obscured it.

Marigold mentally went over her plan. She was banking on the bedroom window at the back still being open. It would be harder getting up the drainpipe in the near darkness, but she was confident she could make it. Making sure that no one was in sight, Marigold stepped over the shallow wall and slipped around to the back of the house. It was even darker here than at the side. She peered up at the windows above and cursed. She was sure that the bedroom window was closed! Marigold patiently let her eyes get accustomed to the blackness. She didn't want to use her torch just yet; the last thing she wanted was for a neighbour to see the light. She eventually realised that her initial impression had been correct. The window was indeed shut. Her mind briefly started to race around the reasons why the window was closed, and who had closed it, before she realised that it wasn't getting her anywhere. If she wanted to gain access to the house, she had to think of something else.

Marigold stood in the darkness and told herself to be logical. What were the other entrances to the house? Of course! The front door had been kicked off its hinges by the men in dark suits only a couple of days ago. Would it have been repaired? Marigold slipped round to the front of her house and stood by the door. From memory it looked to be the same, but it was difficult to tell. Of course, the doorknocker! Marigold reached up and felt the same handle that she'd rapped before. She examined the door more closely, feeling her way more than looking. Large cracks seemed to be near the hinges. Could it be possible that the door had just been put back into place without any repairs? Marigold gently pushed at the right-hand side. With a squeak it moved slightly. Yes! The broken door had just been placed back into its frame to hide the fact that the house was unsecured! Marigold pushed again and managed to open a small gap for herself. She was conscious that the door wasn't properly supported and there was a very real danger that it would come crashing down into the hall again, but nevertheless she managed to open a gap wide enough to slip through.

The interior of the house was in complete darkness. Marigold retrieved the torch from the rucksack she was carrying and risked turning it on. Its pale-yellow beam illuminated the carpet below her in a broad, rough circle. Chips of wood still lay here and there on the carpet. *'Nobody has tidied up too much then,'* Marigold thought to herself. She directed the beam around the walls and up the stairs. She swallowed as she started to climb. She just *had* to see if Dr Black was still there. Step by step she went up until eventually she stood once more before Dr Black's bedroom door. It was only very slightly open. Marigold carefully put her hand on the door and started to push, her heart pumping a little faster now. What would she find inside? Would Dr Black still be on the floor? Would he be on the bed where she suspected the men in dark suits had put him? The door was now open. Marigold raised her torch and swung it around, letting out a sigh when she realised that the bedroom was now empty. In fact, it looked very tidy. The bed had been made, the telephone handset was back in place, and everything looked normal. Marigold stepped inside. She checked that there was nobody standing behind the door, because it seemed like the right thing to do, and then she sat down on the bed, next to the telephone.

Now was the time to check out her idea. She lifted the handset and was relieved to hear the dialling tone humming away. Marigold reached over and pressed the small button marked *redial*. She knew that if the men in dark suits hadn't used the telephone, she would now be dialling the same number that Dr Black himself had dialled the night he died. With her ear against the receiver, Marigold listened to the tones of the number as it was dialled again in some sort of spooky echo from the past. There were eleven digits in total. Marigold now knew that it was unlikely that Dr Black had called the emergency services. If he had, the number would have been much shorter. It wasn't long before Marigold heard a ringing in the earpiece. She waited with bated breath. It rang once, it rang twice… and so it went on. Marigold lost count after the eighth ring. She didn't know whether to feel relieved or disappointed. She was just thinking about putting the handset down when the line was suddenly answered by a woman with a polite voice.

"Hello?"

Marigold's heart started thumping once again.

"Er, hello. Could you tell me who this is, please?" Even as she said it, Marigold kicked herself for sounding so stupid. Why couldn't she have thought of anything smarter to say?

"May I ask who's calling?" said the polite voice, obviously unruffled by the question.

"Er, my name is Anne," said Marigold, lying.

"And what do you want at this time of night, Anne?"

"Um, I wondered if John is in?" Marigold knew that this conversation was going from bad to worse.

"I'm sorry but I think you have the wrong number, Anne. There is nobody here by that name."

"Oh, I'm so sorry to have troubled you. I hope I didn't wake you."

"It is not a problem. Good night, Anne."

With a soft click Marigold heard the receiver at the other end of the line being replaced. She took a few deep breaths. Her plan hadn't gone very well, but at least she now knew that Dr Black appeared to have called a private number on the afternoon that he died. It was unlikely to be a business, unless someone was working late. She consoled herself with the fact that it was at least some progress.

Marigold decided to check the rest of the top floor. She moved silently from room to room, shining her torch around each space as she went. She found nothing that looked unusual, or anything that seemed to be connected in any way to Dr Black's work at the Institute. Each room was sparsely furnished and was exceptionally neat and tidy. Even in the bathroom a neatly folded dry bath towel was laid out over a rail.

Marigold decided to move downstairs. As she descended, she noticed that the light from the torch was fading rapidly. Again, she cursed herself for not properly thinking things through. The torch hadn't been used for some time, and what little charge it had was rapidly draining away.

Marigold stepped into a little room off the hall. It was some sort of lounge. Marigold looked around at the furniture. A comfortable sofa was against one wall. A small television set was in the corner. A low coffee table was in the middle of the room and stacked upon it she noticed a neat pile of magazines. She moved over and flicked through them: there was a TV guide, some gardening magazines and a couple of travel brochures. *'Nothing of any help here'* she thought to herself and went back into the hall.

The next room looked more promising. It seemed to be a little study. A neat little desk and chair sat against one wall and a filing cabinet stood next to the desk. Marigold went over and opened the cabinet drawers. Each one was empty. The first thought that came into her head was that the men in dark suits must have taken the contents. The desk drawer was similarly bare. The light from the torch had now all but gone and Marigold gave it a little shake as if to coax some more life out of it, but the bulb seemed to glow even dimmer.

Marigold sat at the desk. She gave another sigh. This visit wasn't going to be as successful as she had hoped. As she gazed ahead, Marigold noticed the dark outline of a painting on the wall in front of her. She pointed the torch towards it and even though the light was faint she could tell that the painting was full of vibrant colours. But wait; what was that? Standing up, she got the torch as close as possible to the thin lines of white paint that had caught her eye. Marigold peered at the painting. There, painted on the bare chest of a man being burnt at a stake, was an upside-down triangle superimposed over an upright cross. It was the WraithTalker symbol! Marigold tried to look harder at the painting, but the light from the torch finally gave out completely. Marigold thought quickly. Should she risk turning the light on? She decided that she would. The study was positioned towards the rear of the house, and she would be extremely unlucky if a neighbour happened to be watching. Marigold felt her way around the wall to the hallway door. She found a light switch and flicked it. Nothing happened. Again, Marigold uttered a curse under her breath. The electricity must be turned off for some reason.

Marigold stood for a while and thought. She had started to favour the idea of getting the painting off the wall so that she could take it home when she suddenly had a brainwave. Of course! She had another source of light! The WraithTalker machine was quite bright when it was turned on. There would surely be enough light for her to sneak another look at the picture.

Marigold swung the rucksack off her shoulder and untied the straps in the dark. She slipped the WraithTalker out and felt around for the battery compartment. Working from memory, it took her a few moments to find the exact spot. Eventually she pressed on the correct area and she felt the lid swing open. Marigold retrieved the batteries from the rucksack pocket and inserted them into the machine. It immediately sprang into life; the soft blue lights twinkling just as rhythmically as before, when it was last powered up in the churchyard. Marigold was quite relieved to see that they gave out quite a bit of light. She walked back over to the painting and held the machine up to it. By the flickering lights she could see that it depicted some sort of brutal street scene. A man was being burnt at the stake. His bare chest had been daubed with white paint in the form of the WraithTalker symbol and he seemed to be screaming out in absolute terror. A crowd had gathered to watch. Marigold thought that the town looked to be overseas somewhere, and it looked reasonably modern. For some reason she had the impression that the architecture was from the Caribbean. She examined the faces of the people in the crowd. Most people seemed to be smiling, but others seemed to be quite impassive. Marigold initially thought that the impassive people were taller than the rest, but she soon noticed that they had been painted to look as if they were hovering above the ground. Each of them had a faint glow tracing the outlines of their bodies.

Marigold shivered a little. She wasn't sure if it was because she didn't like the painting or because it was getting colder. She put the WraithTalker down on the table and went to sit down on the chair, but a sudden movement in the corner of her eye made her stop and she swung round to look at the doorway. In the faint twinkling blue glow she could just about make out a figure standing there, quite motionless. Marigold gave out a little cry and instinctively took two steps backwards, her hands up to her mouth.

Stammering badly, the frightened girl somehow managed to get a few words out. "W-w-ho's there? C-c-ome forward and show yourself."

The shadowy figure in the doorway stepped forward without a sound. Marigold's eyes widened and she slid her hands even further up her face so that her nose was now also covered. Her eyes stared out over the tips of her fingers and she started to cry uncontrollably, tears rolling down both her fingers and her cheeks. Marigold knew that she had seen this person recently, but the last time was when he had been lying dead in his bedroom upstairs!

THE SPIRIT

It took about a minute for Marigold to start breathing again. The shock of seeing Dr Black standing in the doorway had completely taken her by surprise. Even when she knew that she was thinking clearly again, Marigold found that she was rooted to the spot. Her head was thumping as if all the blood in her body wanted to get out through her ears.

Dr Black stood perfectly still, looking at Marigold with rather a kindly and serene face. Marigold breathed deeply and told herself that there didn't seem to be anything threatening about his appearance. She felt numb and somehow strangely detached from her predicament. Was she dreaming? She took a few more deep breaths and decided that she wasn't.

With a certain amount of reason returning to her, Marigold started to think that the figure standing before her could actually be a living, breathing Dr Black. *'He couldn't have been dead when I saw him upstairs'*, she told herself. *'Oh, my goodness! I've broken into his house!'*

Marigold followed this train of thought until she noticed that she could faintly see one edge of the picture she had been looking at earlier *throug*h Dr Black's body. Marigold licked her lips and started to face her fears. Something was very, very wrong.

Dr Black seemed to be making no effort to speak. Eventually Marigold broke the silence. "H-h-ello," she managed to stammer in a small voice. "I'm sorry for being in your house."

The smile on Dr Black's face widened a little more. There was no other movement and no angry voice. The figure just stood there, looking serenely back at Marigold.

"A-a-re you Dr Black?" whispered Marigold.

The man gave a slight nod. Marigold felt the pressure in her head building up again. It felt like a tuneless orchestra had just been given the order to play a random cacophony of sound. After a few seconds Marigold could take it no more. She had to know.

"Are you… are you… a ghost?"

The figure hesitated slightly before giving another nod. Marigold tried desperately to quell the noise in her head. She breathed deeply again and tried her hardest to regain some sort of composure. She found that she was still rooted to the spot. She couldn't have run now if her very life depended upon it.

The figure of Dr Black raised his left arm and pointed towards the WraithTalker. It was still twinkling away on the table.

"The WraithTalker," breathed Marigold, trying to understand the Doctor's intent. "That is how I can see you?"

Dr Black nodded again. He then held up his other hand, with the palm facing towards Marigold.

"You want me to stop using it?" Marigold said. She felt a little worried. Was she doing something wrong?

Dr Black didn't reply. Instead, he lowered his hand, and then held it up again; this time with his thumb tucked into his palm. Marigold frowned. Dr Black dropped his hand once again, and then held up both hands. This time there was all four fingers and a thumb showing on one hand, and only three fingers on the other. Marigold realised that Dr Black was giving her a sequence of numbers!

"I've got it! You're giving me some numbers for the WraithTalker!"

Dr Black put his arms down and nodded.

"Please start again," pleaded Marigold. "I know what I'm looking for now."

Dr Black duly obliged and proceeded to indicate five, four, eight, eight, one and finally the number seven to the mesmerised girl. Marigold knew straight away that the six numbers must be the settings for the six dials on the WraithTalker. Her brain sent the signal to her legs to carry her towards the machine, but her legs weren't taking orders. To get to the WraithTalker she must pass Dr Black, and she was still very unsure about that.

Dr Black stood and watched Marigold for a while. Eventually, as if he understood her difficulties, he took a step to the side and invited Marigold towards the WraithTalker with a swoop of his hand.

Marigold felt obliged to move, so with feet that felt as like they were walking through treacle she stepped towards the desk and the WraithTalker. She reached the machine without looking at Dr Black. It was taking all her strength to do this simple task. She knew that there was a real chance she would go to pieces again if she glanced at, or even thought about the ghost by her side.

With a practised hand Marigold opened the cover to the battery compartment and slid the holder to one side, just as she had done in the churchyard. The dials were still set to five, five, five, eight, one and nine. Marigold realised that by pure chance the true WraithTalker settings given to her by the Doctor were very close to her home telephone number. She carefully turned the second dial to number four, the third dial to number eight, and the last dial she turned back two notches to the number seven.

"Thank you, Marigold."

The voice by her side came as such a shock to Marigold that she felt as if she'd jumped a little way the right. She risked looking at the figure standing only a few feet away. Even in the soft light Dr Black now looked as if he was very real indeed.

Marigold noticed that she couldn't see through him: his body was completely blocking out the line of the door frame behind. Just for an instant she had an urge to reach out and touch him but then she realised she would be too scared.

"Dr Black. Are you… are you… alive again?"

Even as she spoke, Marigold's head began buzzing with the implications of what she'd just said.

"No, my dear, I'm not," smiled back Dr Black.

Marigold started to feel very vulnerable indeed and she trembled slightly.

"Do not worry, Marigold," continued the Doctor in a soft Scottish accent, "You are quite safe. I cannot touch you and you cannot touch me. The WraithTalker machine is allowing us to communicate, that is all."

Marigold took a few more deep breaths and looked closer at the ghost before her. For the first time she noticed how handsome he was. When she had last been as close as this to the Doctor, all she could concentrate on was his rolled-back eyes and the liquid oozing from his mouth. Now she noticed that short-cropped dark hair topped off an attractive and kind face. Clear blue eyes, the corners of which were creased with smile lines, looked at her affectionately.

"Marigold, I'm afraid that we don't have much time and there are many things that I have to tell you."

* * * * * * * *

Gideon woke with a start in the blackness and wondered for a moment where he was. He tried to move his body, but it felt cramped and stiff. Eventually he managed to stretch a numb arm a little way. He was evidently lying on something hard… ah yes, now he remembered! He was in the hall, by the front door. He had been waiting for Marigold. The hard floor had been unkind to his muscles and the boy just lay there, gently resisting the urge to drift back into an uncomfortable sleep.

And then he heard it. There was a small scratching noise at the wooden front door behind him. He held his breath to listen. Everything was quiet for a while and then the scratching noise started again. Gideon stretched his stiff muscles and propped himself up on one hand. His first thought was that a mouse or cat was outside, but then he noticed that the soft scratching was coming from higher up, near the lock. Someone was trying to quietly get through the front door!

"Marigold, is that you?" hissed Gideon, speaking in a low voice so as not to disturb his mother upstairs. It sounded to the young boy exactly as if his sister had been trying to get the spare key in the lock. The scratching noise stopped. Gideon strained to hear some sort of response. There was no sound for a couple of seconds and then he thought he heard the front gate swinging shut. With some alarm Gideon got to his feet and ran awkwardly into the front room to look out of the window. The front garden and the street beyond were softly lit by the glow of a streetlamp but there was no sign of movement. But someone had been trying to get into the house! He immediately thought of the men in the dark suits and wrap-around sunglasses. Had they finally caught up with the children? He peered out for any sign of a car but could see nothing.

Gideon's legs felt wobbly as he decided to go back and check the front door. Normally it was not bolted, relying on the catch alone for security. Gideon fumbled for the bolts at the top and bottom and gratefully slid them across. With his back leaning against the frame he started to feel easier until he remembered the back door. Marigold must have gone out that way and it was probably open! Gideon darted into the kitchen, not daring to turn on the light. He reached for the key, which was thankfully in the lock, and with trembling hands turned it anticlockwise. It had been unlocked but it was now secure. He also slid the bolts across, top and bottom as before, and breathed a sigh of relief.

Gideon went and sat down in the hall. He glanced at his watch. It was close to two o'clock in the morning. '*Marigold must still be out,*' he thought. Now he had two things to worry about: who had just been at the front door and where was Marigold?

* * * * * * * *

Marigold faced the ghost of Dr Black. As well as feeling nervous, she surprised herself by feeling somewhat excited. She also noticed, for the first time, that the room felt icy cold.

"It's important that you understand a few things about the WraithTalker, Marigold. You must listen to me carefully. The WraithTalker acts as a communications bridge between those who are alive, and those who have been unable, or who are unwilling to make the next stage of their journey," said Dr Black.

Marigold nodded and concentrated as hard as she could. The Doctor continued without pausing. "When I died, I had unfinished business here. My life's work, the WraithTalker, was not complete. I have been trapped in this house for the past few days, unable to leave. It is only now, in death, that I have finally understood what I have been missing. The answer was the WraithTalker tuning or code numbers that I have now given you."

Marigold started to interrupt the Doctor, but he put his hand up to stop her.

"Marigold, I have to speak quickly. I can see that you are intelligent and want to ask many questions, but you must realise that the reason I have been trapped here has now been removed. By setting the correct code for the WraithTalker you have released me. I can now make the next part of my journey. I cannot escape it this time. I can feel it pulling me… and Marigold it feels beautiful."

The Doctor's face lit up with such a warm smile that Marigold felt herself lean towards him a little, almost as if she wanted to share in his happiness.

"We must move along," he continued. "You see me here before you, but I am not a physical thing. I am not real in your sense of the word. The radiation from the WraithTalker is affecting your brain in a subtle way. To help you understand it, think of your brain as being like a radio. Normally it is tuned to a certain range of frequencies, enabling you to see, hear, touch, taste and smell the things that are around you. But it is only your reality. There are other things that exist if only you could sense them or tune in to them. The WraithTalker allows you do this. It tunes your brain to a slightly different frequency. As well as still being in your reality, you are now part of mine."

Dr Black walked around Marigold to the centre of the room. Slightly hesitant of his motives, she tracked his movements by turning around slowly, making sure that she always faced him.

"You will notice that I can walk in the same space as you. This room is as real to me as it is to you. The difference is that I have always been able to see you. Although the WraithTalker allows you to see and hear me, you would not be able to touch, taste or smell me. If you turn the WraithTalker off I will disappear. I will still be here, in a sense, but you would no longer be able to see me."

Marigold felt confused. She tried to sort out the questions that were forming in her mind into some sort of order. "When I first saw you tonight, I could see through you," she said.

"Very likely. The settings for the WraithTalker were not quite correct. You were nearly tuned in to me, but you needed the correct numbers that I gave to you. Do I appear solid now?"

Marigold nodded.

"Good, and you can obviously now hear me, whereas before it would have been very unlikely."

"How do you know my name?" asked Marigold.

"I watched you come in through my bedroom window a couple of days ago. Don't you remember? I heard the boy outside, Giddy you called him, shout up to you."

"Giddy is my brother," said Marigold, remembering the incidents that seemed to have happened such a long time ago now. "Were you already dead when I climbed into your bedroom?"

Dr Black now had an edge of sadness in his voice. "Yes. When you entered I was standing by the wardrobe. I spoke to you, but you obviously couldn't hear me."

Marigold squeezed her lips together and shivered slightly at this news. She remembered that she thought she'd seen something by the wardrobe but dismissed it as a trick of the light. Marigold couldn't help but look sympathetically at the Doctor. She wondered if he had also been looking at his own body, and what it must have felt like.

"I'm sorry," Marigold began, "but I have to ask you this. Did someone… did someone… kill you?"

"Yes, I'm certain I was poisoned. You don't know how strange it is for me to say that. I do not know who is responsible but I have a suspicion. I was so outraged at the injustice that my life was being cut short that I refused to move cleanly on to the next stage of my existence, if I can call it that. Do you understand what I'm saying?"

Marigold nodded and the Doctor went on. "All I knew was that I had to stay and complete my work on the WraithTalker. As I died, I had such terrific insights into where my design was failing. Before I knew where I was, I was trapped in this dimension, unable to move on. The only thing I had succeeded in doing was proving that my theories were correct."

Marigold nodded thoughtfully. She knew that she wanted to ask him a related question but the only thing she could think about was the Red Monk.

"Doctor, my brother and I accidentally caused a ghost to appear in our local church. We were operating the

WraithTalker outside and a lady inside the church saw him. Do you know the ghost? I think he's called the Red Monk."

To Marigold's surprise Dr Black laughed. "No Marigold, I don't know him. I have seen no one else. I cannot move far from the immediate place of my death, and I have only been here for two days. If you hadn't turned up to rescue me I would without doubt have been here for many more days, or even years!"

Marigold felt stunned at this revelation. "So, the Red Monk…"

"… may have been trapped in the church for hundreds of years. Yes, this is very likely I'm afraid."

Dr Black closed his eyes and he seemed to be thinking. When he opened them again there was pure joy on his face. "Marigold, I have to go. There is so much that I want to tell you, to teach you, to discuss with you, but we haven't the time. I will soon be moving on, far beyond the reach of the WraithTalker I'm afraid."

"Doctor, there is so much that I want to ask you," pleaded Marigold.

"I know, my dear."

Dr Black took one step towards Marigold, and she didn't shy away. She no longer felt afraid. She started to reach out but felt awkward. Dr Black smiled.

"I am going now, Marigold. It is the most wonderful feeling. Do not worry. Help your Red Monk, Marigold. He will need your kindness and courage."

Dr Black closed his eyes again and just for a moment Marigold thought that he looked a little fuzzy. She glanced across at the WraithTalker in case it was going dim, but its rhythmic blue lights still twinkled brightly in a most bewitching manner.

Doctor Black opened his eyes again. He had a face of pure joy, but it had a far-off look. "Marigold, you must keep the WraithTalker. Keep it secret and use it wisely. The world is not ready for its discovery yet. Tell him that death is nothing to be frightened of."

With those words the Doctor's body gave a definite shimmer and Marigold found that she could briefly see through the spirit again.

"Goodbye Marigold."

Marigold again moved as if she wanted to reach out and touch the man in front of her. "Doctor Black, don't go yet. There is so much that I want to ask you. Who do you think gave you the poison? Who did you call on the night that you died? Who are the men in dark suits? Where is your body?"

But the image in front of her was now just a pale shadow. The Doctor wasn't even looking at Marigold. She watched him turn and walk through the wall to the left.

"Goodbye," she managed weakly, but the spirit didn't look back.

Marigold had been sitting in the study for some time. The words of Doctor Black still whirled at high speed around her mind, caught up like scraps of paper in a tornado. The WraithTalker twinkled on the desk, although the lights were much dimmer now; the tired batteries were set to expire.

Marigold blinked and realised that dawn must be breaking. The room was starting to get lighter. Patches of brighter grey light were trying to creep around the heavy curtains behind her. Marigold walked over and pulled them back and the soft early morning light flooded into the room. On the far horizon Marigold could see a reddish glow where the sun was starting to climb. The underbellies of some far distant clouds were already coloured in soft shades of pink and orange.

The window was in the same wall that the Doctor had walked through earlier. Marigold noticed the dewy garden outside and wondered where he was now.

Returning to the desk, Marigold retrieved the little notebook and pencil she'd packed into the rucksack the night before. She scribbled furiously, trying to remember what Doctor Black had told her. Her time with him had been frustratingly brief but he had told her some important things. She knew that she had to remember them as best she could.

Gideon woke with a stiff neck. He soon realised that his head was between his raised knees and he lifted it up slowly, smacking his lips as he tried to get some moisture back into his dry mouth.

He now remembered that he had been sitting in the hall, waiting for Marigold to return. He must have fallen asleep.

He glanced at his watch. Half past five in the morning. Where was Marigold? She hadn't come back, at least not that Gideon had heard. He started to worry about her. Where could she be?

Gideon remembered his adventure of the night before. Had he dreamt it? He glanced up the front door: the bolts were still in place. He got up and padded into the kitchen. The back door was also still bolted. Someone had been trying to break into the house last night. It could have been a burglar, but Gideon thought it more likely that it was the men in dark suits. He was very worried indeed. If the men knew where he and Marigold lived there would be no escape. Where could they go? They wouldn't be able to run away from home. The police would *have* to be called now.

Gideon poured himself a glass of milk from the refrigerator and sat at the kitchen table. He was just draining the last drop when he noticed some ginger hair bobbing past the outside window. Marigold! Gideon leapt up with joy and hurriedly unlocked and unbolted the back door. "Marigold! I'm glad to see you!"

"I'm glad to see you too, Giddy," smiled Marigold, giving her brother a little hug.

"I've got something to tell you about last night," he said excitedly.

"And I've got something to tell you," replied his sister. "You had better sit down."

It took about an hour for Marigold to relate her experiences to a stunned Gideon. He occasionally pinched himself to see if he was dreaming. He also looked suspiciously at Marigold at times, thinking that she must be making the whole thing up. But Marigold was so solemn and intense with her narrative that Gideon knew that she was telling the truth.

When she had finished, Gideon found that he had got so many questions that he almost didn't know where to start. "Did Dr Black say what it felt like to be dead," he began.

"Not exactly. He seemed to be stuck in some sort of halfway-house. Somewhere between the living world where we are, and some other place where he was supposed to be."

"Heaven?"

"That's the obvious answer, I suppose, but it may be more complicated than that. Dr Black didn't say where he was going."

"Perhaps he didn't know, but he seemed to want to move on."

"Oh yes. If you could have seen the look on his face he most definitely wanted to move on. I honestly can say that I've never seen anybody look so happy."

Gideon fidgeted in his seat a little. "And he said that you had rescued him?"

"Yes, I think that was the word he used. I think he would have been trapped in the house, haunting it I guess, unable to get free, unless perhaps someone else had got the WraithTalker working."

Marigold's thoughts turned to the Red Monk. She was now convinced more than ever before that his spirit haunted the church; but why? The Doctor had told her to go and help him. Marigold was reminded about something else, and she reached into the rucksack and took out her little notebook.

"The last thing that Dr Black said to me was '*tell him that death is nothing to be frightened of*'," she said, reading aloud part of her notes to Gideon.

"He must have been talking about the Red Monk."

"Possibly, although from the way he said it I had the distinct impression that he was talking about someone else. I mean, why would the Red Monk be frightened of death? He's already dead!"

Gideon shrugged his shoulders. He felt very confused by the whole affair. It was then that he remembered his adventure of the night before. "Oh, I almost forgot to tell you about last night. The men in dark suits and sunglasses tried to break in."

Marigold looked up at once and stared at Gideon in surprise. Pleased that he'd got his sister's attention, Gideon proceeded to tell her about the scratching noise he'd heard at the keyhole.

"Idiot!" said Marigold, after she'd heard her brother's story. Gideon looked hurt. "That wouldn't have been the men in dark suits," she continued. "I've told you before that they'll stop at nothing to get their hands on the WraithTalker. They came straight through Dr Black's door in broad daylight without thinking twice. They'd hardly be scratching at our door lock, and they definitely wouldn't have run off when you called out."

Gideon felt deflated and rather cross with himself. Marigold was right of course. "But who was it then?" he asked.

Marigold looked thoughtful and chewed her bottom lip. "I don't know," she replied. "It's just another piece of the jigsaw."

Just then a sound from upstairs alerted the two children to the fact that their mother was rising.

"Can we go back to bed for a bit now?" pleaded Gideon. "Quick, before Mum notices."

"No," replied Marigold, who, even though she had been up since midnight, felt very fresh indeed. "We've got too much to do today. Anyway, Mum's bound to hear us and we don't want her asking any awkward questions about why we're feeling tired."

Gideon groaned and looked a little fed up. Marigold was right about it being like a jigsaw, he thought. The ghost of a scientist; the ghost of a monk dressed in red; men in dark suits and wrap-around sunglasses; a missing body; unknown telephone calls; someone, or something, scratching at the door in the middle of the night; a strange vicar with an unknown past. Oh yes, there were many pieces of the jigsaw; it was just that Gideon didn't like the picture that was appearing!

"What are we doing today, then?" he asked, almost fearful of the answer.

"Isn't it obvious?" said Marigold, cheerfully. "We've got a Red Monk to visit!"

THE KEY

In the kitchen of the Bennett household Gideon sat munching his way through a bowl of cereal. Marigold nibbled on a slice of toast, whilst her mother was busy making a small sandwich for herself.

"I shall be home early this afternoon, so don't go far today," said Mrs Bennett. "I want you both here when I get back. The forecast is for rain later this morning, so you might as well stay in altogether today."

Gideon glanced over at Marigold. He knew that this wouldn't go down very well with her.

"But Mum," began Marigold, "we thought we'd go and have a look at St Peter's church."

Ruth Bennett looked suspiciously over at Marigold as she cut her sandwich into two. "A church is no place to play, you know."

"We know, Mum. We're not going to play. We just want to have a look round. The windows are so beautiful. I thought I'd take my camera and take some pictures."

"Hmmm, well it might be a bit dull for that, but I suppose you can't do any harm. Just be respectful, that's all."

"We will Mum," smiled Marigold.

Ruth placed her sandwich, together with a banana, into a little plastic container. She gathered up her handbag and swooped across to kiss both Marigold and Gideon on the tops of their heads. "Now remember, I want you home when I get back. You can show me your photographs later. And it will be an early night for both of you; I've never seen two children looking so tired!"

"Bye, Mum," the children chorused together, and Ruth swept out of the kitchen.

As soon as the front door had closed, Marigold turned to Gideon. "Right," she said. "First of all, we're going to need some new batteries for the WraithTalker. The lights were very dim in Dr Black's study. We could go and buy some, but to save time I think we'll use the ones from your little remote-controlled car. I think they're the same size."

"Yes, but…"

"No 'buts' please Gideon. We've got some work to do this morning."

Gideon frowned. "You're determined to talk to the Red Monk then?"

"Yes I am. I've never felt so sure about anything in my whole life."

Gideon thought that he had never felt so helpless in his life. "Marigold, I'm a little worried," he said faintly.

"People are often frightened by things that they don't understand," said Marigold calmly. "Sometimes we just have to be brave." She smiled across at her brother. "It will be fine, Giddy. Listen, you can stay here if you want. I can go by myself."

Gideon perked up. "No way! I'm not letting you do that. I wouldn't be able to keep still. No, I've got to come with you. It's just that I'm a little bit nervous."

"Don't worry. The Red Monk can't hurt us. Dr Black told me that, don't you remember?"

"Well maybe he's got it wrong. Anything could happen. What if we turn into ghosts as well? We could get trapped in the church with the Red Monk."

"Giddy, we would have to die first. Try and think clearly, please."

"All I'm saying is that there is still a lot that we don't know about the WraithTalker. I don't like the fact that signals or radiation or something else coming from it is messing with your mind."

"I know what you're saying, but I trust Dr Black. He told me to help the Red Monk. He said that I had to be courageous."

"You are brave, Marigold the Bold. Perhaps too brave at times."

Marigold didn't appear to hear her brother and started to clear the breakfast things away. "We're going to take some more stuff with us today," she said. "I'm going to take my camera…"

"I thought you were just saying that to please Mum?"

"Partly, but I want to see if we can take a picture of the Red Monk. Also, I want us to take Mum's little dictation machine to try and record his conversations. It's just as well to be prepared. Could you go and find it for me, please?"

Gideon walked off, speaking over his shoulder as he went: "We'd better remember to take a few pictures of the stained-glass windows. Mum said that she would like to see those."

Marigold nodded, although she suspected that the stained-glass windows would be the last thing on their minds.

The two children set off for the church in bright sunlight. The sky above them and to the east was blue, but darker clouds to the west indicated the approaching rain. Gideon wore the rucksack containing the WraithTalker. It now also contained Marigold's digital camera and their mother's dictation machine. They had packed fresh batteries from Gideon's remote-controlled car. Marigold had checked that they had powered up the WraithTalker before storing them away.

"Keep your eyes peeled for any sightings of the men in dark suits and sunglasses, or their car," said Marigold, glad to be out in the fresh air again. She had started to feel a little sleepy and heavy-headed in the house.

Gideon nodded and dutifully looked over his shoulder every few steps. "We can't go on like this," he complained, "watching our backs every time we go out."

Marigold looked at her brother's dejected face. "We'll sort something out soon," she said. "I promise."

The pair walked along in silence for a while, and it wasn't long before they turned the corner into the road where St Peter's church stood majestically.

"One of the things I don't understand," began Gideon, "is how people can see ghosts without a machine such as the WraithTalker. I mean, the Red Monk was apparently seen about seventy years ago."

"I've been thinking about that," replied Marigold. "Now that we know that there *are* such things as ghosts, I think that many of the stories we hear of their sightings are actually true. Some people are probably predisposed to seeing them. Do you remember what Dr Black told me about the fact that your brain needs to be tuned into them?"

Gideon nodded.

"Well, I can only assume that the genetics or something of some people mean that they are more likely to see them. Perhaps other conditions can affect it as well, like an electrical storm. Lots of people seem to see ghosts when there's a thunderstorm."

"In the movies," said Gideon. "I'm not sure about real life."

Marigold gave a little laugh. "Yes, you're right. But something else has just occurred to me. Lots of people see ghosts, but I've never heard of anyone holding an intelligent conversation with one like I did. Although, thinking about it, spiritual mediums claim to hear voices if the conditions are right. They don't usually see their ghosts, though. Hmm, certainly the WraithTalker seems to create the right set of sight and sound conditions for anybody who is within range of it."

Gideon thought that this all sounded reasonable. "I wonder what the range is?"

"It was far enough to affect Mrs Appleby through a thick stone wall," said Marigold. "But I don't think it could go much further. After all, the machine is only powered by a couple of small batteries and your remote-controlled car only works over a short distance."

The children had reached the front wrought iron gates of the churchyard. Beyond them a short path led prettily to the church. It was along this path that Mrs Appleby had run after she had so unexpectedly been confronted by the Red Monk two days ago.

Marigold stooped and smiled at her brother. "Are you ready?"

Gideon took a deep breath and smiled back. "As ready as I'll ever be."

The two children started down the path. They hadn't taken many steps before Gideon noticed something. "Hey Marigold, look over there. Isn't that Harold?"

Marigold squinted against the sun in the direction that her brother was pointing. A hunched figure was standing near the far side of the graveyard, looking down at something. Marigold recognised the dull grey raincoat instantly. "Yes, it is. Let's go over and see him. We don't want him disturbing us when we get into the church."

With Marigold leading the way, the children stepped out over the grassy churchyard in the direction of the road sweeper, negotiating the lumpy ground and a variety of headstones on the way.

"Hello Harold," called out Marigold, as the children got close.

Harold lifted his head and looked at the children, blinking a little. "Oh, hullo Marigold, Giddy,"

Now that they were next to him, Marigold noticed that he was standing in front of a small shiny black headstone. It had gold lettering marking the simple words: '*In Loving Memory of Susan Gilliard, passed peacefully away August 14th 2010. RIP.*'

"It's my wife. I often come here to stand awhile," said Harold solemnly.

"Oh," said Marigold. "I didn't know that you had been married."

"Yes, to the sweetest and most gentle woman who ever walked this Earth. She was a lovely lady."

Marigold knew from the date on the headstone that Harold's wife had died young.

"I'm sorry Harold. We'll leave you in peace. Giddy and I are here because we want to look around the church."

"Ghost hunting for your school project?" queried Harold.

Gideon immediately shot Marigold a glance, but all she did was smile at the road sweeper. "Something like that. We've brought a camera to take a few photographs. Do you know if the church will be open?"

Harold looked thoughtful. "I dunno. It's usually locked up… but you could get the key…" and with that Harold suddenly stopped and his head turned back to his wife's grave.

"Get the key?" queried Marigold.

Harold squeezed his thin lips together and they quickly turned white. It was as if he didn't really want to say any more, but after a short moment he did continue. "I was just going to say that you could get the key from the vicar, but remember what I was telling you yesterday. He's a strange character and I would stay away from him if I were you."

"I think he's nice…" began Gideon, but he was swiftly interrupted by Marigold.

"Thanks Harold. We'll just go and look to see if the church is open. Are you staying here long?"

Marigold was anxious to find out if there was any chance of the genial road sweeper following them into the church.

"No, I've got to get some work done," replied Harold, much to Marigold's relief. "I've received word that the inspector's doing his rounds. I want to look busy."

The road sweeper fixed Marigold with his warm brown eyes. "Just be careful you two. Remember; don't get mixed up with the vicar if you can help it."

Marigold stared awkwardly back at him for a while, unable to take her eyes off his cruel-looking mouth for some reason. She eventually gave him a nod. The children bade the road sweeper farewell and turned back to drift towards the church.

Harold looked at his wife's grave. It wasn't long before he was lost in his own thoughts again, but then a slight movement over to his left caught his eye. He was sure someone, or something, had just moved behind a large stone monument a few metres away. Harold fixed his gaze on the impressive structure, which stood about three metres high and about the same distance around, and waited for any further signs of activity. All was quiet. A white stone angel mounted on top of the monument peered back at the road sweeper with cold, unblinking eyes. Harold glanced quickly over in the opposite direction and saw Marigold and Gideon busy at the front door of the church. He turned to the monument and crept as silently as he could up to its base. Still there was no sound or any other evidence that there was anything there. Keeping close to the stone, Harold inched his way around until he could lean over and look right behind the ancient structure. His eyes widened.

"I thought it might be you," said the road sweeper, chuckling. "You'd better get back. I think you're about to have a couple of visitors."

Marigold and Gideon stood before the big wooden front door of the church.

"Well, here goes," said Marigold. She turned the big iron ring of the door handle and pushed hard. The door didn't move. She even put her shoulder against it. After a couple of attempts Gideon pushed as well, but it was to no avail.

"It's locked," said Marigold, and she uttered a curse.

Gideon looked around. "What do we do now?"

"Let's try the side door; the one that the vicar normally uses."

Gideon nodded and the two children slipped around the side of the church. This area was still in shadow. It was cooler round here and Gideon secretly hoped that this door was going to be locked too. He was pleased, then, when Marigold pushed against the oak structure and it also wouldn't move.

"Oh well, I suppose we better go home," said Gideon, trying to sound as if he was disappointed.

Marigold gave him a withering look. "We're not finished yet. As Harold said, the vicar must have a key. Come on!"

Marigold strode over the grass towards a small wrought iron gate set into the stone wall that separated the vicarage from the churchyard. Gideon broke into a trot to catch up with his determined sister.

Outside the vicarage, Marigold skipped around to the front door and gave it a couple of knocks. After a few moments she knocked again. Gideon was just starting to worry that Marigold would be looking for open windows to climb through, when the noise of the door being unlocked stopped him.

The door swung open, and the Reverend Orle stared at the children. He looked hot and flustered and Marigold thought that he had a rather cross expression on his face, but it quickly disappeared.

"My, my, if it isn't the children from the church," he smiled. "Little Gideon, I shall never forget your name, and Marion, no, sorry, Marigold!"

Gideon beamed back at the vicar and Marigold started to speak. "We're sorry to trouble you vicar…"

"No, no, not at all. Please, do come in."

Marigold looked at Gideon and then followed in the footsteps of the tall man, who had rapidly disappeared into the blackness of the house. The two children proceeded down a long dark corridor, carefully avoiding small tables and chairs that seemed to have positioned to trip up the unwary.

Eventually they were led into a room that was filled with the light from some open French windows.

"I've just been in the garden, pruning the honeysuckle," said the vicar.

Gideon noticed what appeared to be a big glass of white wine on a desk and wondered if the vicar had been drinking the night before.

"Now, what can I do for you two?"

He smiled at the children and Gideon couldn't help but smile back. He liked this genial giant of a man.

"We wondered if it would be OK if we borrowed the key to the church for a short while," began Marigold.

The vicar flinched slightly but he continued smiling. "And why would you want to borrow that, may I ask?"

"Er, I'd like to take some pictures of the stained-glass windows.

"It's for a school project," she added, conscious that she'd used this same excuse several times now.

"I see," said the vicar, and he turned around with his head bowed. Marigold knew that he was thinking, and she also knew it was going to be bad news.

"I'm sorry," said the vicar, turning back. "I'm keeping the church locked up for the time being. That business with Mrs Appleby, you know. I've had a lot of curious people hanging around."

"But all we want to do is to take a few photographs," pleaded Marigold.

"That's as maybe, Marigold, but I'm not going to change the rules for anyone. I'm sorry. Maybe if you came back on Sunday morning, after service. I'll be glad to wait with you whilst you take some pictures."

Marigold thought quickly. She knew that this wouldn't be satisfactory at all. If she and Gideon were to contact the Red Monk, they would have to be alone.

"Thank you for your offer, vicar," she said, "but I think we shall be busy on Sunday. Perhaps another time."

The vicar nodded, smiling. "Yes, it's a shame but many people seem to be busy on a Sunday these days." He then turned his attention to Gideon. "It looks as if you're well packed up there, Gideon. Are you going on a hike or something?"

Gideon gaped back at the vicar. He knew he couldn't say anything about the WraithTalker and was grateful when Marigold quickly butted in. "My camera equipment is in the bag," she said somewhat truthfully.

"Oh, I see," said the vicar, who was still looking intently at the rucksack.

Marigold decided to change the subject quickly. "We heard about what Mrs Appleby saw in the church, vicar, and as you know we saw you in there shortly afterwards. Did you notice anything unusual?"

The vicar turned to look at Marigold. "No, I didn't. Everything was very quiet. I shouldn't really be telling you this, but it would appear as if Mrs Appleby has been working a bit too hard just recently. She thinks she saw something, but I'm convinced it was a shadow or a trick of her imagination. She says that she never wants to step back in the church again, but I've told her to take a couple of weeks off. I think she'll rally round. She's much too good a cleaner to lose just like that!"

Marigold smiled back at the vicar, although secretly she was disappointed at not gaining access to the church. "Thank you for your time," she said. "I hope we didn't disturb you."

"No trouble at all, Marigold. I'll show you the way out."

The vicar led the children back down the dark passageway. Just before they reached the front door he spoke again over his shoulder. "I suppose that your mother knows what you're up to this morning?"

"Oh yes, she knows that we're here," replied Marigold.

"That's good. Well, perhaps I'll see you both in church sometime?"

The vicar beamed at the children as he showed them out. They smiled politely back until the front door closed with a heavy click. Gideon let out a big sigh. It was mainly out of relief, but he tried to make it sound like disappointment.

"Well, we're well and truly stuck now," he said. "The church is all locked up and the vicar won't open it. A small army couldn't get past those heavy wooden doors. We stand no chance. We can't go in through the stained windows, not unless you want to destroy some priceless history. What are we going to do?"

Marigold stood and chewed her bottom lip. For once she was stuck. How could she persuade the Reverend Orle to part with his key?

Gideon, meanwhile, was kicking a few tufts of new-mown grass on the vicar's lawn, near a bush with large yellow leaves. He suddenly gave a yelp. "Of course!" he exclaimed. "We could always use the other key!"

Mrs Appleby's house was a neat little semi-detached house in a street near to where Marigold and Gideon lived. Her garden was a tidy spectacle of colour. Plants of every size, shape and colour combined to give such a wonderful display that the local paper had once kindly called it *'the best-kept garden in Avonmead,'* much to Mrs Appleby's great delight.

Marigold and Gideon stood at her front gate, looking at a crazy-paved pathway that twisted its way through the colourful borders.

"As a cleaner, she's bound to have a key," said Gideon, still proud that he'd managed to think of something before Marigold.

"I think you're right," agreed Marigold, "and she wouldn't have dropped it off with the vicar when she left the church, because she was in such a state of panic and fear; it's a question of whether or not the vicar has been round to collect it and I suspect that he hasn't."

Marigold opened the neat little gate, and the children wove their way through the colourful borders to Mrs Appleby's front door. Marigold rang the doorbell and Mrs Appleby answered it almost immediately.

"Oh, my dears, come in, come in. It's so nice to see you."

Mrs Appleby stood to one side, allowing the children to step politely into her house. Mrs Appleby was a short, wiry woman in her early sixties. She'd let her hair go naturally grey and she peered at the children with dark shining eyes.

Her hall was small and bright; crammed full of what Gideon later called 'knick-knacks'. Dark narrow mahogany shelves were everywhere: over the radiator, on the walls, even above the front door itself. Resting on the shelves were what seemed to be hundreds of little china figures and pieces. Some were just of bunches of flowers; others were of women clutching flowers to their breasts; yet more were of wheelbarrows full of flowers.

Gideon didn't know where to step next and found himself on tiptoe. He was trying to avoid bumping into Marigold and Mrs Appleby, and at the same time he had the uneasy feeling that he was going to knock into some shelves, bringing hundreds of priceless china pieces smashing down around them.

"Go through into the lounge, Gideon," pointed Mrs Appleby. "Go on dear."

Gideon half leapt into the room that Mrs Appleby had indicated. Marigold and Mrs Appleby followed.

"Sit down dears. Now, that's better. Would either of you two like a drink? I can make some tea, or I think that I've got some orange squash somewhere."

Both children politely refused. Gideon remembered back to the last time he'd had some orange squash at Mrs Appleby's. It had tasted old and musty back then, which must have been more than a year ago. He suspected that she'd still got the same bottle.

"And how is your *dear* mother," continued Mrs Appleby. "I don't know how she copes with you two; mind you, you're not a bit of trouble, are you?"

Marigold and Gideon dutifully shook their heads. Marigold decided that this idle chit-chat had gone on for long enough. "Mrs Appleby…"

"Yes, dear?"

"We were very sorry to hear of your experience in the church."

The smile on Mrs Appleby's face dropped for a moment before she forced it back up again. "Yes, well, the less said about that whole episode the better. I don't want to talk about it dears, if you don't mind."

"But may I ask you what you saw?" persevered Marigold.

"Nothing dear. Nothing to worry your little head about. Now are you sure you wouldn't like some orange juice?"

Marigold sensed that they wouldn't be getting any more information from Mrs Appleby. She obviously still thought that the two children were younger than their years. *'If only she realised what we are trying to do,'* pondered Marigold, but she knew that it would be a mistake to talk about the WraithTalker.

"Mrs Appleby, we were talking to the vicar today, the Reverend Orle. He explained how upset you'd been. We thought that it might be a good idea if we returned your church key to him, to save you the trouble."

Marigold hoped that this would do the trick. If Mrs Appleby suspected that the children were really on a mission from the vicar, she might hand the key over. Mrs Appleby's face dropped again, and she looked a little worried; even disappointed.

"Yes, well, of course the vicar will want to find another cleaner, for the short term at least, so I suppose I had better let him have the key back. I'll go and get it."

Marigold and Gideon grinned at each other, but Marigold quickly sobered up when she heard Mrs Appleby talking to herself as she hunted for the key.

"Now where did I put it… oh dear I thought it would be here… or maybe here… oh no, don't say that it fell out; it could be anywhere. Oh dear, I don't know what I'm going to do. I loved that little church. Oh dear, I wonder if the vicar's angry with me. Why would he be angry with me? Why wouldn't he come and see me himself? Now where is that key?"

Marigold hadn't anticipated that Mrs Appleby would be upset if she had to give the key back. She started to feel guilty, but at the same time she was worried that Mrs Appleby had mislaid the key for good. Gideon was thinking no such thing. He sat fidgeting on his chair, looking nervously at a row of china ornaments next to him.

"I've got it dears!" called out Mrs Appleby from the next room, and she shuffled back in. With her head down she went straight to Marigold and placed the key very deliberately in her hand, folding Marigold's fingers around it. Marigold could tell that she was upset, and her heart reached out to her.

"Thank you, Mrs Appleby. If it's any consolation, let me tell you that you might be doing some poor soul a great service by letting me take care of this."

Mrs Appleby looked at Marigold with moist eyes and a slightly puzzled look on her face.

Marigold and Gideon walked back to the church in silence. Light rain had now started to fall, and the sky had completely clouded over, making the neighbourhood look quite gloomy. Marigold chewed her bottom lip, deep in thought. Gideon couldn't stop thinking about the coming adventure. Was there really the ghost of a Red Monk who haunted the church?

The two children crept up the pathway through the churchyard. They kept a watchful eye for both the vicar and the men in dark suits. The children didn't particularly want to bump into the vicar after he had forbidden them unaccompanied access to the church. Marigold also scanned the graveyard for Harold. There was no sign of him. He must have returned to work as he had said.

At the large front oak door to the church Marigold eased the key into the lock. It turned surprisingly easily. The rain was coming down heavier now and the two children were glad to slip inside. Marigold closed the door behind her.

"Don't lock it!" pleaded Gideon. "We might need to make a quick exit!" He was somewhat reassured by the thought that he could run faster than Mrs Appleby.

The children stepped quietly and slowly up through the nave. There were no lights switched on and with the cloudy skies outside it was particularly dark and gloomy inside the church.

"Here; this is about the place where Mrs Appleby saw him," said Marigold as they reached the front pew. "Let's get set up."

Gideon slipped the rucksack off his back and Marigold took it from him. She removed the WraithTalker, the batteries, her camera and her mother's dictation machine. Marigold lined them all up next to each other on the first pew, making sure that they were all within easy reach.

Marigold then did something that made Gideon feel very uncomfortable. She left him sitting on the front pew and walked to the front of the church, at the head of the nave. Almost as if she were addressing an imaginary congregation she turned and shouted aloud.

"I'm not sure if you can hear me. I think that you might be able to. I just want to talk to you. Do not be frightened; I want to try and help you."

Gideon trembled on his seat. "Marigold, you're frightening me," he whispered, his mouth suddenly feeling very dry indeed.

Marigold only smiled gently and walked back towards her brother. "Put the batteries in the WraithTalker, Giddy. I've told you before, there's nothing to be frightened of. Dr Black said that ghosts cannot hurt us."

Gideon wasn't convinced. His hands shook slightly as he opened the battery compartment and inserted the batteries. As he did so he half thought about asking Marigold if he could wait outside but he knew that, terrified as he was, he couldn't leave her now.

The WraithTalker twinkled into beautiful life once more. Gideon let his hand rest over the compartment just in case he wanted to remove the batteries again in a hurry. He kept his head down, hardly daring to look up. He half expected the Red Monk to have materialised on the pew next to him, but he could see nothing when he sneaked a look.

"I can't see him," said Marigold. She was standing in front of her brother looking towards the back of the church, peering into the darker corners. She shivered slightly, sensing that the air had somehow got cooler. Gideon slowly raised his head. Marigold watched his expression change from someone who was worried, to someone who looked as if he was in a deep shock. Gideon tried to speak but could only make a dry popping noise with his lips. Marigold knew that the ghost was standing behind her, somewhere over her right shoulder. She turned around slowly.

There, behind the raised pulpit, stood the Red Monk. His hood was up, covering his face apart from the thin line of his mouth. Marigold took a deep breath. The ghost didn't seem very happy to see the children.

THE RED MONK

The Red Monk raised his hands and slipped his hood back, slowly revealing the whole of his head. He peered at Marigold and Gideon in an inquisitive way, although his lips remained in a tight line.

Marigold sensed that her breathing was much faster now, but she didn't feel frightened, or at least that is what she kept telling herself. Gideon was petrified. He stared at the man behind the pulpit with a mixture of fear and awe. This was a real ghost! Gideon was gripping the front edge of the pew he was sitting on so hard it was starting to hurt his fingers.

The Red Monk looked as if was in his early forties. Close-cropped black hair topped off a serious but intelligent looking face. He was quite thin and his sunken eye sockets seemed to accentuate his black eyes, which still stared at the children.

Marigold was about to issue a greeting when a movement from the monk stopped her. He had turned and was climbing down the steps of the pulpit. He reached the bottom, and the children had a good view of his scarlet robes. Marigold was amazed at the richness of the red colour. The WraithTalker was working perfectly, she thought. The ghost in front of her appeared perfectly solid; absolutely nothing was visible through him.

"My, my, my. This is very interesting," said the Red Monk, walking towards Marigold. "Yes, it is, I say to myself. Are you some sort of angel?"

The monk stopped and turned to Gideon. "And what about you. Are you some sort of angel too?"

Marigold felt uncomfortable that the monk was talking to Gideon, who she sensed, quite correctly, was sitting absolutely terrified behind her.

"Hello. We mean you no harm. And no, I'm afraid that we are not angels," she admitted.

The Red Monk turned back towards Marigold. "Then why do your bodies glow and shimmer as they do? Very strange I say to myself. Very peculiar it is to my friends too."

Marigold felt a little confused. Glowing? Shimmering? Friends? Marigold looked around for any other spirits, but she could see nothing.

"So, if not from God, are you from Satan?" asked the Red Monk, squinting at Marigold in a suspicious manner.

"No… no… we are definitely not from Satan. We want to try and help you."

The Red Monk looked puzzled. "But you are glowing and shimmering. How are you going to help me? And do I need helping? What help can you give me? Very strange this is I say to myself."

Marigold turned round to look at Gideon to see if his body was glowing in any way, but he looked completely normal to her, apart from the fact that he was staring goggle-eyed at the scene in front of him.

Marigold thought quickly. She reasoned that it was quite likely that the WraithTalker was also affecting the Red Monk's perception in some way. Perhaps people who could now see him appeared to be glowing to him.

"Have you seen anybody else glowing and shimmering?" she asked.

"Sometimes I do and sometimes it's not very strong and other times it comes and goes, but you two are almost on fire! Brighter even than the flower lady!"

Marigold immediately realised that the flower lady must be Mrs Appleby. Marigold thought about explaining the

WraithTalker to the monk but thought better of it. She wasn't sure that he'd understand.

Without another word the Red Monk turned and walked off towards the side of the church. At the wall he swung towards the back, looking up at the little stained-glass windows above him as he went.

"I'll be asking my friends about this," he said. "I will, and I don't know what they'll be saying about it all. No, I don't. I don't know what they'll be saying about all the glowing and shimmering. Maybe they will like it and maybe they will not."

Marigold was starting to realise that being alone for such a long time had probably driven the poor man quite mad. She turned towards her brother. "Giddy, get the dictation machine working and record his voice. Take a few pictures as well. I'm going to follow him."

Gideon, who seemed to have lost all power of movement apart from turning his neck to follow the movement of the Red Monk, sprang into life and started fiddling with the dictation machine.

Marigold stepped after the Red Monk. "Where are you going?" she called out.

The Red Monk stopped under one of the little stained-glass windows at the side, showing interest in a particularly kind-looking saint. "If angels don't glow and shimmer then what things do, Paul? It's a mystery and it's a worry. There's no doubt about it."

The Red Monk then stepped off in another direction, which caused Marigold to stop in her tracks. He was walking straight through the wall of the church! It wasn't like the other evening when the half-shadow of Dr Black seemed to melt through the wall as he left; the Red Monk seemed capable of walking through the wall as if it wasn't there! Marigold dashed to the spot where he'd disappeared.

"Come back, please!" she shouted. She half thought about running outside to see if he was in the graveyard, when suddenly the monk reappeared a few feet away. He was now underneath the next stained-glass window. He was still looking upwards and talking to himself.

"If it's help I want then I'd better get help, Thomas. But what help is it that we need? Do you know what help it is? All the glowing and shimmering is no help at all."

The monk continued to walk to the back of the church. He had just reached the corner when Marigold called out.

"Stop! Please stop! I need to speak to you."

The Red Monk stopped in his tracks and turned towards Marigold with an inquisitive look on his face. She hurried over to him. There was a flash and Marigold realised that Gideon had taken a picture. The Red Monk glanced back at Gideon, but his expression didn't change.

"What is your name?" asked Marigold.

"My name? Oh my, my, my. What is my name? I can't remember my name. I can remember the names of my friends, but I can't remember my own name."

Marigold looked with sympathy at the monk before her. "You haven't spoken to anybody in a long time, have you?"

The Red Monk looked at Marigold and she noticed his dark eyes twitching. He looked as if he was going to say something but then he wandered off again, this time to look at the most impressive arched stained-glass window at the back of the church. He started talking to himself again as he looked up. "My friends are Matthew and Mark, and Luke and John and many others. Don't know what help we need. All this shimmering and glowing. That's no help. My name is no help, is it?"

Marigold noticed that he was talking to an image in the large stained glass above him. She realised with a shiver that these flat glass figures were probably the oldest friends that he had, if you could call them that. The names he was giving were the names of the saints in the windows.

There was another flash and Marigold knew that Gideon had taken a new picture. She just hoped that the dictation machine was working. There was so much that she wanted to ask the ghost next to her.

"Please," she began, "please… it's important that I ask you some questions."

The monk didn't react to her; he just carried on looking up at the impressive arched stained-glass window high above, muttering something more quietly to himself now.

Marigold didn't feel deterred. She knew that if she and Gideon were to help this poor soul, they had to find out some more information, especially concerning his death. Marigold decided against engaging him with any pleasantries. She would get straight to the point.

"I have to ask you this. Did you die here?"

The Red Monk swung round to look at Marigold. He moved his head forward to peer at her more closely. She noticed a deep suspicion in his eyes. Marigold thought fast; her current tactics were getting her nowhere. She decided that she had to take a chance.

"I must tell you the truth now," she began, staring straight back into the Red Monk's face. "I *am* an angel, of sorts. I have indeed come to rescue you."

The ghost continued to peer at her for a few seconds and then he turned once more to look up at the stained-glass window.

"I knew she was an angel. With all that shimmering and glowing," he said. "Matthew told me she was an angel and Mark said that she might help me. But I don't know what my name is. I wonder what my friend the son of Simon, the son of Robert, the son of Christopher, the son of James, the son of Thomas would say?"

The monk turned back to look at Marigold. This time there was some softness in his voice. "I thought that your shimmering and glowing would help me."

He looked at Marigold expectantly. She didn't hesitate with her question: "Were you killed here?" she asked.

The monk paused for a while, never taking his eyes off Marigold.

"Here I was," he said pointing to the spot where he was standing, "and my leg was hurting, and I woke up and they cut me and they cut me. I knew that you'd help me with all your shimmering and glowing. I knew that an angel was here."

"Why did they cut you?" asked Marigold, with a genuine gentleness.

"They cut me and they cut me, and I tried to call out to the Lord Abbot but he wasn't there. Only Matthew, and I couldn't tell Matthew, although Matthew knew. Yes, Matthew knew but he wouldn't help me. Even when they were cutting me. But I knew you'd help me with all your shimmering and glowing."

Marigold thought fast. She imagined the poor monk being cut somehow, possibly right on this very spot. She also thought back to what Dr Black had told her about his being trapped as a spirit because he had unfinished business. What unfinished business could this poor monk have had, to stop him moving cleanly to where he was supposed to go?

"What did you try to tell the Lord Abbot," Marigold asked.

"His treasure of course. I'd hidden his treasure. But I didn't see him, I only saw Matthew and I was cut and cut. I can't remember my name. But I knew you were an angel. Your shimmering and glowing told me."

"What was his treasure?" persisted Marigold.

The Red Monk turned and took one step over to the back wall. He rested his outstretched arms against it and allowed his head to drop quite loosely between them, as if he was trying to think.

"The treasure. I'd hidden his treasure. Somewhere. I can't remember where. Matthew saw them cut me and I knew you'd help me. I thought that you were an angel."

There was another flash as Gideon took a photograph.

"I think we've got enough pictures now, thanks Gideon," said Marigold, not taking her eyes off the ghost in front of her.

"Was it big treasure?" she asked, stepping over softly to stand next to the Red Monk.

"Big as an egg it was. Or maybe smaller. Or maybe bigger. I can't remember. It was his red treasure and I had to hide it. I can't remember my name, but I knew you were an angel."

And without warning the Red Monk suddenly disappeared. Marigold blinked, almost as if she couldn't believe it. Where had he gone? She didn't have time to think about it, because she suddenly became aware that Gideon was running at full speed down the centre aisle towards her!

"Someone's coming," he hissed. Marigold noticed that he had precariously gathered up the equipment and the rucksack in his arms. She dashed straight for the front door of the church and swung it open for Gideon to charge through. She pulled it closed behind her and locked it before tearing after her brother down the church path.

It wasn't until they reached the road and she caught up with a gasping Gideon that he was able to explain: "I heard someone coming in through the back of the church," he panted. "It sounded like a door being unlocked. It must have been the vicar. I ripped the batteries out from the WraithTalker because I didn't want him seeing the Red Monk, and then I scooped up everything and ran."

Marigold looked at her brother in amazement. "Giddy, that was brilliant!"

Gideon let out a huge sigh-come-laugh that also let Marigold know that he was very glad indeed to be away from the church, even if they were now standing out in the pouring rain.

It was late afternoon, and the children were in Marigold's bedroom. Gideon sat quietly on the bed whilst Marigold worked at a little desk, tapping away on her computer. She was anxious to display the images that Gideon had taken with the digital camera. After a few minutes the first one came up on the screen. To her surprise, and to Gideon's when he had leaned forward to look, she could see herself on the picture but there was no sign of the Red Monk.

"I'm sure he was standing about *here*," she said, pointing to an area of the screen near to where her image was.

"Yes, he was," said Gideon, puzzled. "I remember worrying that he was going to be hidden behind you when I took the picture."

"Let's look at the others."

Marigold proceeded to bring up the other two images. In each case the figure of Marigold could be seen, but there was no sign of the Red Monk. Marigold chewed her lip as she looked at the pictures. On the last photograph there was an impressive view of the arched stained-glass window at the back of the church. Marigold could be seen standing sideways to the camera, looking intently at something.

"The Red Monk was definitely standing *there*," she said, pointing to an area of the screen. "I was staring at him leaning against the wall as you can see. But there's absolutely no sign of him."

"We couldn't have dreamt it all, could we?" said Gideon, pinching himself.

"No..." said Marigold, "but I think I'm beginning to understand. Pass me the dictation machine, will you?"

Gideon dutifully picked up the little recorder from the bed and handed it over to Marigold. She played it at high speed until a high-pitched chirping sound told her that there was a voice. She pressed the play button, and the children heard the faint sound of Marigold's voice: '...*What did you try to tell the Lord Abbot?*'

Both children strained to hear the Red Monk's reply, but there was nothing apart from a slight electronic hiss. Marigold turned the volume right up so that the hissing noise became much louder, but there was still no indication that the Red Monk was speaking. Gideon thought he heard whispering but told himself it must be his imagination. After a couple of seconds Marigold's voice could be heard again, this time much louder: *'What was his treasure?'*

Marigold switched the dictation machine off. She was still chewing her bottom lip and Gideon thought it best not to interrupt.

"Dr Black told me that the WraithTalker affected our brains in some way," she said eventually. "It tunes them in to a different frequency or something, allowing us to see and hear ghosts. But of course, the camera and the dictation machine…"

"Have no brains!" finished Gideon, suddenly understanding it.

"Yes, they only record what is our normal everyday view of things. The ghosts only exist in our minds."

Gideon screwed up his face a little. He thought he understood, but it was difficult.

"Don't worry about it too much," said Marigold. "We've more important things to think about. I was really hoping that we could help the Red Monk this afternoon. We've *got* to help him to move on to the next stage of his journey, like Dr Black."

"Do you think it's the treasure that's held him back?" asked Gideon.

"I'm almost positive. He showed us where he died in the church and I'm pretty sure he was murdered from what he said. He was trying to tell the Lord Abbott where he'd hidden some treasure. That *has* to be the reason why he's trapped in his current existence as a ghost. He never passed on his secret."

"But he told us that he couldn't remember where he'd hidden the treasure," complained Gideon.

"I know. The poor man can't even remember his own name. I'm afraid that if we're to help the Red Monk we're going to have to find his treasure and that's going to be a big problem for us."

"As if we haven't got enough to worry about at the moment," groaned Gideon.

Marigold didn't reply. She had subconsciously started to chew her bottom lip again.

Gideon also sat quietly for a while and then he looked puzzled. "If the monk has been around for a few hundred years, why doesn't he talk like they used to in the olden days? I would have expected him to say *'thee'* or *'thy'* or *'sire'* or something."

"I think it's because he's been able to see and listen to people the whole time he's been a ghost," said Marigold thoughtfully. "Doctor Black told me that he could see and hear me, even though I couldn't see him. The Red Monk must have listened in on tens of thousands of sermons in the church, and even more conversations amongst the congregation. As time has gone by his language has evolved with the people he's listened to. He only speaks a bit funny now because very few people have spoken to him, if any at all. You saw how he talked with the saints in the stained-glass windows. Those images are the only things that haven't changed over all the time he's been a ghost. At some point he must have started talking to them for company and it's been that way ever since."

"He was calling them by name," said Gideon. "You know: Paul and Matthew and so on."

"Yes, those must be the names of the saints," replied Marigold. "I recognise them as names from the Bible, but at one point he said something that I didn't understand. It was something about one of his friends being *the son of Simon, the son of Robert, the son of Christopher*, and so on. I suppose it's got some significance but I've no idea what it means."

The children sat for a while, both feeling deeply sorry for the lonely monk. Gideon couldn't even begin to imagine what it must be like to see people, but for them not to be able to see or hear you. He could well understand how it could drive you into having glass images for friends.

"He thought we were angels," said Marigold. "Our bodies appeared to be glowing to him, which I think is some side effect of the WraithTalker. He also knows that we can see and hear him, so he realises that we're different. I'm sure he thinks we've come to rescue him."

"I just hope we can," said Gideon with a touch of poignancy.

Marigold stood up and had a stretch. "It's no good," she sighed. "I'm going to have to have to have a good long, hard think about everything. At these times Sherlock Holmes liked to be left alone with his pipe and his violin. I think I need to be left alone with a glass of milk."

Gideon took the hint. "I'll fetch you one," he said, "and then perhaps I ought to run down to the shop and buy some more batteries for the WraithTalker. I'm worried that those from my radio-controlled car will soon be flat."

"That's a good idea. Thanks, Giddy," smiled Marigold. "We just don't know when we might need the WraithTalker again. We'd better be prepared, so get two sets. Here's some of my pocket money to pay for them."

Gideon disappeared and after a few minutes he returned with a tall glass filled with milk. "Mum says that dinner will be ready in one hour. I'll be back from the shop in ten minutes, but I won't disturb you."

Marigold smiled her thanks and took a sip from the glass.

Gideon strolled down the street, whistling softly to himself. Although the image of the Red Monk had initially been very scary for him, the brave and calm way in which Marigold had dealt with the spirit had given him a little courage. Even so, he still wasn't sure that he'd like to face the Red Monk by himself.

Gideon found that he couldn't help thinking about the treasure that the Red Monk had mentioned. What was this treasure? Was it buried in the churchyard? Gideon grimaced at the thought of digging in the churchyard and uncovering lots of old bones to find it. But what could the treasure be? The monk had mentioned a red treasure; however, he'd seemed uncertain of its size. Could it be a red leather casket filled with gold coins? Gideon started to dream about holding the coins up and letting them slip through his fingers and he subconsciously whistled a little louder, which was unfortunate because it meant that he didn't hear the car pull up alongside him until it was far too late.

Marigold lay on her bed, still turning the events of the previous few days over in her mind. She was amazed when she realised that she was completely comfortable with the idea of ghosts and the concept of the WraithTalker machine. It now all seemed completely natural and logical, whereas a couple of days ago she knew that she would have looked very cynically at anyone who had seriously talked about ghosts. Her experiences, first with Dr Black and now with the Red Monk, had left her feeling very comfortable with the spirit world. Marigold thought that perhaps she had been lucky so far. Could there be anything such as an evil spirit? She thought back to the painting in Dr Black's study. It had depicted a crowd watching a man being burnt at the stake. Marigold shivered and she decided to turn her thoughts to other questions. Who had murdered Dr Black? Why had he been murdered? Was it someone who was after the WraithTalker? Who had he telephoned as he died? The woman at the other end of the telephone had sounded very polite. What connection had she got to Dr Black? Where did the men in dark suits and wrap-around sunglasses fit in? Were they really after the WraithTalker? If not, why were they chasing her and Gideon?

Marigold felt that she was going round in circles with these questions, so she turned her thoughts back to the Red Monk. She had the feeling that she was missing something, but what was it? She knew that her instincts were rarely wrong. Marigold stood up and reached for her electronic tablet. Maybe if she found out a bit more about monks and monasteries it would help. Lying down on the bed, she browsed through a few search pages and soon found an appropriate web site. Her eyes widened as she read the following passage about the dissolution of the English monasteries:

At the beginning of the 16th Century, monasteries owned over a quarter of all the cultivated land in England. Farmers who rented the land from the monks often criticised them for being greedy and uncaring landlords and it was often claimed that the monks had been corrupted by their wealth. This was not always justified as many monasteries used their resources to help the sick and the poor in their area.

In 1535, King Henry VIII ordered his Vicar-General, Thomas Cromwell, to carry out an audit of the monasteries, which he did with four men in just six months. Cromwell reported 'manifest sin, vicious, carnal and abominable living is daily used and committed amongst the little and small abbeys.' As a result of this audit King Henry VIII ordered the dissolution of the monasteries, starting with the smaller ones.

In April 1536 there were over 800 monasteries, abbeys, nunneries and friaries. Just four years later there were none.

Marigold thought for a moment. She was sure that St Peter's church had been built on the site of a monastery. She made a mental note to search out Harold again tomorrow. He would probably know something about the history of St Peter's. She was certain that certain sections of the church were part of the original monastery. Surely that was relevant! Marigold went on with her reading.

Thomas Cromwell and his soldiers persuaded many monasteries to close voluntarily. Those that didn't were forced to hand over their property and treasures on pain of death. Some monasteries, especially if they housed a religious shrine, had become very prosperous. Wealthy pilgrims often gave expensive jewels and ornaments to the monks that looked after them.

Marigold had read enough. She lay back on her bed and started to think. It was highly likely, she reasoned, that the Red Monk had been a monk in the monastery that had stood on the site of St Peter's church. She realised with a tingle what the implications of this were. The monk had probably haunted the site for about five hundred years. This was a bit longer than she had imagined. With nobody to converse with over that period, it was no wonder that he was behaving in such a strange manner.

Marigold turned her attention to the death of the Red Monk. He had mentioned being cut quite a few times. Marigold imagined the poor man being attacked, probably with a sword or a large knife. The way that he had repeated his words, she imagined him being subjected to quite a frenzied attack, although she couldn't be certain of this because he had often repeated himself with other parts of the conversation.

Marigold remembered what the monk had said about the treasure. He had hidden it somewhere, but he'd now forgotten where it was. Marigold had the impression that the treasure had belonged to the Lord Abbot, and she let her imagination run free for a while, trying to invent a story that fitted the facts. It wasn't long before she sat bolt upright on the bed. Of course! The Lord Abbot had got a treasure, probably given to him by a wealthy pilgrim, and the Red Monk had hidden it when Cromwell's soldiers had called. He had been unable to let the Lord Abbot know where it was hidden because the soldiers had cut him down and killed him. The monastery must have been one of the places that had resisted the dissolution! Marigold tingled. She had a story that fitted the facts of the case so far. But it still meant that the treasure had to be found.

"Marigold, your dinner's ready!"

The call from her mother broke Marigold's concentration.

"OK, Mum. Coming!"

Marigold ran downstairs, feeling quite pleased with her investigations. This was short-lived, though, at the next words from her mother.

"Where's Gideon?"

Marigold felt as if her heart had dropped through her body and down a deep dark pit, which was threatening to suck down and consume the rest of her body too. "Isn't he back yet? He went out to buy some batteries about an hour ago."

"I haven't seen him," said Mrs Bennett, trying to keep calm.

Marigold was already on her feet. "I'll run down to the shop..."

"But what about your dinner?"

"Put it in the oven," called back Marigold over her shoulder. She raced out of the house so fast she didn't even stop long enough to close the front door.

Running down the street Marigold could only think of one thing. The men in dark suits and wrap-around sunglasses had captured Gideon. Marigold cursed herself again and again as she ran. Why had she let him go out alone? She ran down the few streets she knew Gideon would have taken. There would have no reason for him to take any other route. With each corner she turned she hoped to see her brother strolling towards her. Each time she was disappointed. Marigold started to pray. She hadn't been a particularly religious person in the past, but she prayed as hard as she could now. She found herself thinking that she'd do anything if Gideon could be safe and well. If only she hadn't investigated the scream at Dr Black's house. If only she hadn't picked up that briefcase. Marigold thought she had been so smart and brave, but right at this moment she had never felt so insignificant and so much out of her depth.

Marigold burst into the little shop where she knew Gideon would have bought the batteries. "Has my little brother been in here?" Marigold gasped at the young girl on till.

"What does he look like?" replied the girl, sensing Marigold's anxiety.

"Small. Red-headed like me. He would have been in here sometime within the last hour."

The girl screwed up her face as she thought. "Nope. Sorry. I've been here all afternoon; there's been nobody in the shop like that."

For the second time in a few minutes Marigold felt her heart plummet to her feet. Without a further word she turned on her heels and raced home, frantically calling out Gideon's name as she ran. By the time she reached the house, she was sobbing uncontrollably. Marigold stumbled into her mother's arms and looked tearfully up at her anxious face.

"He's gone, Mum. I just know that he's gone!"

REVELATIONS

"Are you sure you haven't seen Gideon?" asked Ruth Bennett. She was a few streets away from home and had bumped into Harold. It was one of those rare occasions when Harold had got his broom in his hands; he'd been doing a little sweeping at the roadside.

"I'm sorry, Mrs B," said Harold. "I saw the kids earlier. Didn't they both come home?"

"They did, but then Gideon popped out. That was over an hour ago."

Harold squeezed his lips into a grim line and shrugged his shoulders. "I'll keep an eye open for him. If I see him, I'll send him straight home. I'm sure he's just got waylaid somewhere."

"Possibly, although it's so unlike him. I can tell you that I'm starting to get quite worried now. I've searched quite a bit. I think I'll go home and call the police."

Harold nodded and started stroking his broom over the ground. Ruth had half hoped that the road sweeper would take more interest, but he seemed a bit cold and surprisingly interested in his work. Without another word she turned and hurried off.

As soon as Ruth Bennett was out of sight, Harold stopped working and tied the broom to his cart. Leaving it standing at the side of the road, he strode off purposefully towards the church.

* * * * * * * *

Marigold sat chewing her bottom lip, staring at the telephone. Her mother had left the house five minutes ago to look for Gideon and she'd ordered Marigold to stay in the house in case either he returned, or someone rang.

Although Marigold had been praying for it, it came as a complete surprise when the telephone did ring! She dived for the handset and pulled the whole unit onto the floor with a crash. Marigold hoped desperately that she hadn't cut the caller off.

"Hello?" she asked expectantly.

"Marigold?"

"Gideon! Is that you?"

"Yes…"

"Where are you?" cried Marigold with such relief. "We've been so worried about you. Mum is out looking…"

"I'm OK. Please just listen for a moment. I'm at the church. I think I've solved the Red Monk's secret, but you have to come here now and bring the WraithTalker."

"Come home first, Giddy. Mum's been so worried…"

"No, you have to come now. It's… it's important that you come right this instant. I'll explain everything when you get here. You will bring the WraithTalker won't you? *Please*, Marigold."

Marigold was so happy to hear from Gideon that she felt that she'd do anything for him. "OK. Stay where you are. I'll write a quick note for Mum, although I might pass her on the way. I'll see you in a few minutes."

"Thanks Marigold," and with that Gideon hung up.

Marigold hurriedly scribbled a note for her mother and pinned it up on the front door: '*Gideon safe and well. Gone to fetch him. Back soon. Love Marigold XXX*'

Marigold grabbed the rucksack containing the WraithTalker from her bedroom and once again ran from the house. '*What could Gideon have discovered?*' she wondered, although to be honest she didn't really care; she just knew that she had to get to the church quickly to see her brother.

Marigold stood panting at the entrance to the churchyard, leaning on the wrought iron gate for support. She had run all the way and she was exhausted. The church itself looked very quiet and still. Where was Gideon? He must be in the church itself, she thought.

Marigold pushed open the gate and walked down the path. She hadn't seen her mother on the way. By now she hoped that she'd had read the note on the door and wouldn't be worrying. Marigold reached the front oak door of the church and tried the handle. It was unlocked! She started to push the door open, but even as she did so she started to get very suspicious. In her excitement and relief she hadn't been thinking clearly, but now, as the door creaked open on its hinges, Marigold's mind moved into top gear. Why had Gideon gone off by himself to the church? That was certainly out of character. He wouldn't risk meeting the Red Monk by himself, Marigold was sure of that. If he had genuinely solved the Red Monk's secret, he would have come back home to tell her. She started to have an awfully bad feeling about this, but she wasn't allowed to dwell on it for too long because the old oak door was now wide open. Marigolds eyes bulged and her mouth dropped: Through the archway she could see the Red Monk! He was sat facing away from Marigold on the back pew. His hood was up. There was no sign of Gideon and Marigold started to feel very uneasy indeed. She had the WraithTalker on her back; she could feel its weight and she was sure it hadn't got any batteries in it, so how could the Red Monk be visible? Marigold's instincts screamed at her to turn and run, but she knew that she couldn't: Gideon was here somewhere, and she sensed that he needed her. She had to go on.

Marigold stepped slowly forwards towards the Red Monk. He didn't move at all. *'Perhaps he hasn't heard me?'* she thought, her mind still whizzing around the possibilities. Should she turn the WraithTalker on? He would surely hear her then, but why could she see him without it? She moved closer, not daring to speak. The monk had been so talkative before. What was wrong now? Even his robes seemed to be duller.

Marigold was now standing right behind him. She took a deep breath. "Hello," she whispered. "It's me again. Your angel."

The figure in front of her turned around slowly. "Hello Marigold."

Marigold's hand went up to her mouth in shock and she gave a little shriek, trying to comprehend the person in front of her. It was the Reverend Orle! He slowly got to his feet, slipping his hood down to his shoulders.

"Come with me," he said grimly. "I'll take you to Gideon."

Marigold followed him like a little lamb. She had been taken completely by surprise and for once was lost for words.

The vicar led her out of the church by the side door and over to the vicarage. Marigold looked around for signs of another soul to call out to, but there was no one. Marigold tried to think clearly but her fear clouded her thoughts and she felt confused. Why was the vicar dressed as the Red Monk? Was he really taking her to Gideon? How much did the vicar know? Perhaps his intentions really were honourable?

At the vicarage the Reverend Orle opened his front door and pushed Marigold inside with a rough shove. There was no doubting it now! Marigold knew she was in grave danger.

"Go down to my study," ordered the vicar with menace in his voice. Marigold felt her way down the dark corridor, avoiding the items of the vicar's furniture as she had done before.

'I've got to think! I've got to think!' she told herself. She felt in mortal danger, and she was extremely worried about Gideon. She pushed the study door open and to her delight the first thing she saw was her brother!

"Giddy," she cried out in relief, rushing over and flinging her arms around him. Gideon was sitting on a chair and Marigold quickly saw that his hands were tied behind his back. He had been crying and on seeing Marigold he started up once more.

"I'm sorry, Marigold," he sobbed. "They made me do it. I had no choice."

"Don't worry, Giddy," I'm here now, said Marigold still hugging her brother tightly, although it quickly registered with her that he had said *'They made me do it.'* Who were *'they*?' Letting go of Gideon she turned around just in time to see the Reverend Orle closing his study door. Sitting behind it had been another person: Dr Elizabeth Whitehead!

"Hello Marigold," she said with a false smile. "Glad you could join us." The Doctor turned to the vicar. "Can't you stop that boy crying?"

"He'll shut up now," said the vicar, fixing his eyes on Gideon who immediately looked down, avoiding the vicar's stare. His crying quickly dried to a sniffle.

"What do you want with us?" cried Marigold, suddenly feeling truly angry and a whole lot braver.

The Reverend Orle seemed to ignore her and walked calmly over to his desk. "Sit down, please Marigold," he said, indicating a chair with a swoop of his arm.

The chair was next to the big ornate fireplace, and it was only then that Marigold realised that the room was extremely hot. A fire burned in the grate and a poker rested with its tip in the embers.

'*If they've been threatening Gideon with that...*' thought Marigold grimly. She clenched her fists tightly as she sat down.

"You probably realise by now why you're here," said the vicar, sitting down behind his own desk.

"The WraithTalker," said Marigold, although she had to unclench her teeth to say it.

"Yes, that's right. I take it that it's in your rucksack right now?"

Marigold nodded. She had forgotten she was still wearing the rucksack. In all the excitement it had felt as light as a feather. She glanced across at Gideon. He still had his head bowed and the anger rose in Marigold once more. "You won't get away with this," she found herself saying.

"Oh, I think we will," the vicar chuckled. He had now unlocked his desk drawer and Marigold saw him remove a small velvet drawstring bag. He opened it in silence and took out a glass phial containing some orange liquid.

Marigold knew that she ought to be in a state of panic, but her anger had clarified her thinking. She knew that she had to buy herself and Gideon some time to give them an opportunity to escape.

"I suppose that's the poison you used on Dr Black," she said.

The Reverend Orle looked up with a smile. "Why yes," he said smoothly. "Very well deduced, Marigold. Except that it's not quite true to say that I was the one to use it. My lovely assistant here," and at this point the vicar gestured over to a smiling Dr Whitehead, "had plenty of opportunity to give it to him at the Institute."

"I suppose the poison comes from Africa," said Marigold.

The vicar looked more surprised now "You have got it all worked out, haven't you Marigold?" he said darkly. "Yes, this liquid comes from Africa. If one uses two or three drops, it's quite an illuminating and addictive substance. I'm quite partial to it myself. Anything over ten drops is completely fatal, with the benefit of a delayed action of course."

Marigold turned to Dr Whitehead. "So, you gave him a lethal dose at the Institute. He went home feeling ill and… and… he died at home all alone."

Elizabeth Whitehead smiled back at Marigold without flinching. She has magazine cover looks, thought Marigold, but her eyes now betrayed her. The blue was ice cold.

"And all because you wanted the WraithTalker," continued Marigold, fixing her eyes back on the Reverend Orle.

She noticed, with some alarm, that the vicar had set two large crystal goblets out neatly in front of him. He dripped some of the orange liquid into each of them; Marigold couldn't be sure, but it was at least twelve drops into each.

"Yes, Marigold. All because of the WraithTalker. I don't suppose you fully appreciate what you've got there."

"Oh yes, I know what I've got here..." she began.

"NO, YOU DO NOT!" shouted the vicar, rising to his feet, almost toppling the chair behind him. He stared angrily at Marigold, the reflection of the open fire burning angrily in his eyes.

Marigold felt shaken for a moment before she felt the defiance rising in her once more. "I know that I've got something that Dr Black wanted to be used for decent purposes," she said firmly, matching his fierce gaze.

The Reverend Orle gave a little chuckle. His face softened and he stepped away from his desk. Marigold glanced across at Elizabeth Whitehead and noticed that she was looking at the vicar with a mixture of fear and awe.

The Reverend Orle took a box of matches and lit the candle on his desk. He proceeded to move around the room, slowly lighting the others. Marigold counted seven in total. The vicar talked as he worked: "How well do you know your Bible, Marigold?"

"Fairly well, I think," replied Marigold, anxious not to show any signs of weakness.

"Pah! I doubt if you know much more than a few parables! I'm talking about the *real* Bible. The Book of Revelations, and others not included by Athanasius. The story of things to come, not events that happened thousands of years ago!"

Marigold kept quiet, watching the vicar light another of his candles.

"You think you're clever, don't you Marigold?" sneered the vicar. "If you're so smart, perhaps you could tell me what *eschatology* means to you? Do you even know what it is?"

Marigold shook her head.

"It's the theology and philosophy concerned with the ultimate destiny of mankind," said the vicar. "You might call it the End of the World. Surely you've heard of that?"

Marigold nodded.

"Well, it will be soon upon us, with all its glory. Quite simply, on the Day of Judgement the dead will once again rise with the rest of us, and we will all be taken into Heaven. Now just imagine, Marigold, just imagine that we could talk to the dead. Would that not be them rising again? Would that not be the precursor to the Day of Judgement? Those who have lain asleep for so long: for hundreds, for thousands of years even. What if we gave them a voice again?"

Marigold stared at the vicar. She realised now that he was totally and utterly mad. "I think you have misunderstood death…" she began.

"MISUNDERSTOOD!" thundered the vicar again, turning angrily towards Marigold.

"You don't frighten me," said Marigold calmly.

After a few moments the vicar gave another half-smile and moved over to stand behind his desk. He lifted a glass decanter of water and proceeded to half fill each goblet of poison. Marigold noticed that Gideon had turned his head to the side and was looking in abject terror at the crystal glasses.

Marigold's mind raced round the possibilities. She could run off towards the door, but Dr Whitehead would surely stop her before she reached it, and what about Gideon? His hands were tied behind his back but at least his feet were still free. He could run, but she would have to guide and balance him. She glanced across at the French windows. They were shut and presumably locked. She could grab Gideon and try to charge through them, but they looked sturdy. The pair would probably only end up in a heap on the floor. She suddenly remembered the poker. Could she have the courage to lift it up and strike both the Reverend Orle and Dr Whitehead with it? She doubted it, but it might be her only option. She mentally went through the scenario: she would attack the vicar first, but he would undoubtedly block the first blow and Elizabeth Whitehead would be on top of her before she could try again.

Marigold subconsciously chewed her bottom lip. What could she do? Time was running out.

"And now the WraithTalker please Marigold," said the vicar. "I want you to show me how it works, and then I want you to hand it over to me. We will then toast the future with a nice glass of wine."

"You will never have the WraithTalker," said Marigold angrily. She just *had* to stall the vicar somehow.

"Oh yes I will, my dear. I found that young Gideon here was most co-operative when faced with a red-hot poker. I know that you will be too!"

"Alright, alright," said Marigold, noticing that the vicar had started to rise out of his seat. "I'll tell you everything that you need to know. But first, I have a few questions for you. Could you satisfy my curiosity for a couple of minutes, please?"

The vicar leaned back in his chair and put his fingertips together as if in thought, or it might even be prayer, thought Marigold.

"Charles, let's get on with it," urged Dr Whitehead. "We have to leave this evening."

"Shut up!" snapped the vicar, and Dr Whitehead immediately bowed her head. "It will be interesting to hear how much the children have worked out."

Marigold licked her lips. She knew that she had to keep talking.

"Well, first of all, I suppose that the robes you are wearing are from your time in Africa."

"Yes, Marigold. I'm very impressed. Please continue."

"I think that they probably weren't always that colour. I would guess that you dyed them when you came to St Peter's."

"Correct again, Marigold. When I heard about the legend of the Red Monk it seemed like a nice touch."

"The thing I don't understand is how you knew that Gideon and I had the WraithTalker."

Marigold thought that she knew the answer to this, but she just wanted to keep the vicar talking.

"That was easy, Marigold. When Liz couldn't find the WraithTalker at the Institute we suspected that it was at Dr Black's house. I went there to search for it but could find nothing. Not a trace. Even his papers had gone. I presume that you've got those as well?"

Marigold nodded, but immediately started to think that this was a new twist. Who had got the papers?

"We then had a fortunate breakthrough," continued the vicar, glancing across at Dr Whitehead, "when you turned up at the Institute and seemed extremely interested in the work being carried out. You were also spending a lot of time hanging around the church and even wanted to get access. Don't you remember? It's a pity that your red hair is so distinctive, Marigold. Liz and I soon realised what you were up to. Gideon was wearing that rucksack on his back the last time you were here. It wasn't difficult to deduce what he had in it."

"And having found out where we lived, one of you tried to break into our house last night to steal the WraithTalker," said Marigold.

"Yes, Liz tried to get it. A noise from the boy here frightened her off, though."

Marigold thought quickly and then nodded towards Dr Whitehead. "So, I assume that you and Liz are… are…"

To Marigold's surprise the Reverend Orle laughed.

"Yes, you could say that Liz and I are *very* good friends. As one of my most loyal parishioners we have had some, er, interesting discussions about the meaning of life and what we both want from it."

Marigold glanced towards Dr Whitehead again and noticed a slight look of anxiety and even embarrassment in her face.

"Charles…" she began.

"Yes, my dear, we had better be moving on…"

"There is just one more thing," interrupted Marigold. "Did you find Dr Black when you searched his house?"

The Reverend Orle looked back at Marigold and smiled.

"Yes, my dear, I did. He was tucked up nicely in bed, poor thing. I thought it best not to leave him lying around so I've got him upstairs. He's hidden in a cupboard."

Marigold's blood froze. She looked at the vicar's calm, smiling face and she knew right then that there was nothing, absolutely nothing that this man wouldn't do to reach his twisted ends.

"And now for the WraithTalker," he said.

Marigold saw that his eyes flashed with excitement. Her heart started to sink. She had failed to think of anything.

Slipping the rucksack off her back, Marigold removed both the WraithTalker and the batteries. She turned the box over so that the battery compartment was facing her, and she pressed on the surface once more, perhaps for the final time Marigold thought, allowing the lid to swing up. She sensed that the vicar and Dr Whitehead had both moved closer to get a better look. She slipped the batteries into place and closed the lid. The WraithTalker twinkled into life and Marigold looked again at the pretty dancing blue lights before her.

"Give it to me," commanded the vicar, rising from his seat and holding out his hands.

Marigold glanced across at Gideon. His head was hung low, and she noticed a silent tear rolling down his cheek. Gideon obviously felt his sister's gaze because he lifted his head. The two siblings looked at each other for a few short seconds. Gideon read the look of fear and hopelessness on his sister's face. He changed his expression and Marigold immediately caught the meaning: *'Don't give up on us now!'*

Marigold looked down at the carpet for an instant and then she raised her head towards the vicar, speaking slowly with deliberate venom through her clenched teeth. "I said that you would NEVER have the WraithTalker!"

With that Marigold leapt up and threw the box as hard as she could into the open fire! It hit the back of the grate with a crash, splitting open instantly. The plastic casing must have been made of something extremely flammable because it flared up immediately with a blue *'whoosh'* that even caught the angry girl by surprise.

"NOOO!" screamed the vicar, and he leapt round his desk to the fire. Marigold stood back and watched as he desperately tried to retrieve the WraithTalker from the flames, failing miserably as his hands got burnt time and time again. Marigold knew that she had got her diversion! Now was the time to get Gideon out!

But before she could do anything, a strange sight befell the room. Seemingly from out of the fireplace and the raging inferno of the WraithTalker stepped the Red Monk! He walked forward from the wall with an eerie silence. Marigold recognised him at once in his bright scarlet robes. His hood was up and his mouth was grim.

The vicar fell back in surprise and scrabbled away as best he could on all fours. Dr Whitehead leapt up and screamed loudly, falling back into the corner of the room.

The Red Monk stood there and slowly removed his hood. "All this glowing and shimmering. What is going on I ask myself. I see my angels and I see the others. Matthew does not like it. No, he does not. And I do not like it either!"

Dr Whitehead screamed so loudly that Marigold thought that her eardrums were going to burst. The Reverend Orle had reached his desk and had grabbed a bible from the top.

"Who a-a-re you?" he stammered.

The Red Monk fixed the Reverend Orle with his black eyes. "My name is Ezrael."

The vicar looked terrified. "The Apocalypse of Peter... the Angel of Wrath!"

Marigold stopped listening. She had her diversion and she knew what she had to do. Grabbing Gideon by his upper arm she dragged him to the study door. Flinging it open she started down the dark corridor. She glanced behind her, fearful that the vicar would be giving chase, but the Red Monk had moved across to stand in the doorway, blocking it completely. He was looking at the vicar and Dr Whitehead. As Marigold turned she heard the monk starting to say, "You're glowing and a shimmering as well, but I know that you are from the devil…"

Marigold and Gideon negotiated the long, dark hallway and burst out of the vicarage. Marigold was half-dragging and half-guiding Gideon who still had his arms tied behind his back. Racing down the drive, the children had almost reached the road. Marigold had a flickering sense of freedom, but it was to be short-lived. From out of a clump of yellow-leaved bushes, three muscular men in dark suits and wrap-around sunglasses stepped forward and held the two children in vice-like grips. Marigold went limp under the strength of the arms holding her. In an instant a black Mercedes had raced up and skidded to a halt. The two children were swiftly and roughly bundled into the back. The three men also dived in and the car roared off, its tyres smoking.

ZARATHUSTRA

All was peaceful in the windowless room. The old man lay patiently in bed, the bright crystal light from the chandelier overhead barely troubling him at all.

He saw big yellow leaves all around him. Through a gap in the foliage he could see the spire of a honey-coloured church in the near distance.

"Shall we go in?" asked a calm disembodied voice.

The old man was considering his reply when another disembodied voice, this time speaking with more urgency, interrupted his thoughts. "Wait! There's something happening. Look!"

The old man spun around and came out of the leaves. He could see a path and all at once he could see the children. They looked shocked and they looked terrified. The old man gave a little smile. He'd got them now!

* * * * * * * *

Harold peered out from the large, flat tombstone he'd been hiding behind in the graveyard of St Peter's church. He'd seen Marigold and Gideon come rushing out of the vicarage. It had almost been as big a surprise to him as it had been to the children that several burly men in dark suits and wrap-around sunglasses had leapt out of a large yellow-leaved bush in the vicar's drive.

Harold watched as the children were forced into the back of a big black car. He tried desperately to catch sight of the car's registration plate as it sped away, but it couldn't be seen. He uttered a curse under his breath and turned his attention back to the vicarage. He was sure he could still hear screams. Harold set his mouth into a grim line and decided to sit tight.

* * * * * * * *

It wasn't long before the black Mercedes left the leafy suburbs of Avonmead. It continued to travel at high speed through the surrounding countryside. Inside the car Marigold and Gideon were wedged firmly between two burly men on the back seat. Two more sat in the front. Gideon still had his hands tied behind his back and was feeling rather uncomfortable. The disappointment of being captured again had been a big shock to him after the brief elation of the escape from the vicarage.

Marigold was gravely concerned. She had realised that the men were making no attempt to conceal the route the car was taking. In her mind this could only mean one thing: it didn't matter if the children memorised the journey or not, because they would not be allowed to lead anyone else here. She tried to keep a watchful eye on all the turnings that the car made, mentally trying to go over the route again and again to keep it fresh in her mind; however, she eventually realised that she had forgotten a part of it. So now she had a new strategy where she remembered shorter sections, each starting with a landmark. Currently they had turned left, right and second left after passing a place called Cray Farm.

The two siblings hadn't spoken to each other and had barely exchanged a glance. Gideon was now quite alert. Marigold sensed that he had an air of defiance about him. Feeling comfortable with her scheme for remembering the route, Marigold steeled herself and turned her thoughts to escape. Could she and Gideon dive out of the car when it came to rest somewhere, perhaps at a junction? She doubted it. The children would have to get past one of the burly guards, and she knew from how she had been manhandled into the car that the men were extraordinarily strong. Besides, Gideon still had his hands tied behind his back. Even if she managed to escape it would be hard to get him away as well, and there was no way that she was going to leave her brother. Could the children call out for help or wave at someone? Marigold thought that this could be a possibility, but it would have to be done discreetly which was almost impossible given her current position. She shifted slightly in her seat and moved her right hand so that it was now resting on her lap. Gideon had helped by leaning gently away from her. Good! He seemed to realise that she was getting ready for action. What signal to the outside world could she make? Marigold thought long and hard and decided that the only thing she might be able to do would be to dive into the front of the car and pull hard on the steering wheel to make the car veer off the road and possibly crash. This would have to be a last resort, but she knew she could do it if she had to.

The men in dark suits had also sat in complete silence as the car had sped along. Marigold had a three-quarters rear view of the head of the front passenger, and so for the first time could get a discrete look at one of the people who had been so anxious to get hold of the children, or more accurately she thought, the WraithTalker. Marigold gave a little shiver. What would these men do when they found out that the children no longer had the machine? She had of course thrown it onto the fire at the Vicarage. Her thoughts turned back to Reverend Orle and Dr Whitehead. Were they still in the study with the Red Monk? She clenched her teeth as she remembered the two glasses of poison that the vicar was about to force them to drink.

Marigold once again concentrated on the front passenger. He seemed to be in his mid-thirties and had a well-groomed muscular appearance. His black hair was short at the sides and slightly spiky on top. But even as she studied the man, she realised that she felt very tired. The events of the past few days, coupled with the motion of the car and the fact that she hadn't had much sleep last night, were finally taking their toll. If only she could doze for a while. Marigold bit her bottom lip hard. She had to stay awake! She had to remember the route! She looked more intently at the man and wondered what Sherlock Holmes would have worked out from what he saw. There were probably hundreds of things that could be deduced, but she couldn't think of one. Why were the men all wearing sunglasses? She had to think!

Marigold woke and realised that the car was coming to a crunching halt. She blinked rapidly, trying to come to her senses as quickly as possible. She glanced down at her watch. Six o' clock! She must have been asleep for more than ten minutes! Marigold wondered where they were now. All she could see through the front windshield was trees.

The car's rear door opened with a soft click and warm summer air swept in, mixing deliciously with the air-conditioned cool air from within the car. The man to Marigold's left got out and she felt obliged to follow, as did Gideon, shifting along the seat as best he could with his hands still tied behind his back. As the children moved, Gideon managed to whisper "I've memorized the route" into Marigold's ear. Marigold showed no reaction as she stepped out onto some soft yellow gravel. She blinked as she comprehended the vista: a large house, more castle than anything else, loomed over them, sweeping away to the left and right in irregular structures that included two tall round towers. Marigold didn't really have time to take it all in before a woman in a smart grey suit came running towards them from out of what was evidently the front door: a large opening set between two pillars that were supporting a large stone canopy.

"Come on, come on. Oh, you poor dears! What have those beasts been doing to you?"

Marigold was slightly taken aback by the welcome. The woman approaching them was about fifty years old, of medium height but of rather a large build. She had silver hair brushed neatly back and tied in a bun. The woman went straight over to Gideon and looked at his bound hands.

"What's happened here?" she shrieked. "Untie the poor boy you brutes!"

The four men in dark suits, who were still wearing their wrap-around sunglasses, looked at each other for a couple of seconds before one of them moved over to pull at the ropes that bound Gideon's wrists. In a few seconds he was free, rubbing his sore and cramped limbs with a pained expression. Marigold instinctively went over to her brother and examined his injuries: his wrists were very red but did not appear to be cut.

"Those brutes have got no sense at all," said the woman, scowling at the men in sunglasses. She put her arms out to usher Marigold and Gideon towards the house. "Come on dears, I've got a drink and a snack all prepared for you, and of course you'll want to call your mother."

Marigold was so surprised at this last sentence that she stopped in her tracks and had to be urged forward again by the woman in the grey suit.

"Come on, come on. Let's get inside and away from those thugs."

"Did you say that we could call our mother?" asked Marigold feebly, hardly daring to hear the response.

"Yes of course you must, or your father, it doesn't matter which."

"We haven't got a father," said Gideon, "or should I say that he left us when we were young."

"Oh, the brute!" shrieked the woman again. "Well then, you'll have to call your mother, won't you?"

Entering the house, the siblings stepped into the most ornate entrance hall they had ever seen. It reminded Marigold of one of the rooms in Hampton Court Palace which she had once visited on a school trip. Gilded picture frames housing elaborate oil paintings of every size hung on the walls. A rich red carpet covered the floor and swept up an unfeasibly wide staircase which split off in three different directions near the top. An immense crystal chandelier sparkled overhead, its complex light beautifully illuminating the reds and the golds of the room.

'*This room is bigger than our house*,' thought Gideon as he looked around.

"Can I ask where we are?" queried Marigold, not yet willing to believe that she and Gideon were safe.

"Why yes; you're in Mr Zarathustra's residence. He's had you brought here because he wants to talk to you. I think that you and he have a lot to talk about, don't you?"

Marigold looked intently back into the clear blue eyes of the woman in the grey suit. "Does that mean that we are free to go if we wish?" she asked.

"Oh yes, er, but I wouldn't leave just yet, because Mr Zarathustra has gone to a lot of trouble to find you." The woman leaned forward and whispered to Marigold as if someone might be listening: "I'd just have a quick word with him if I were you. He likes to get his own way, you know. That's why he employs those thugs," and with that she gave her head a nod back in the direction of the front door.

"Alright," said Marigold. "But we will call our mother now, and you must give us the address of this house and the telephone number, so that she can call us back to verify that it's the right number."

"Of course, of course. All this fuss!" said the woman speaking aloud again and rolling her eyes back up into her head.

Marigold thought that there was something vaguely familiar about her, but she couldn't quite put her finger on it.

* * * * * * * *

From his hiding place behind the tombstone Harold peeked out at the scene before him. Three policemen and a policewoman were leading the Reverend Orle and Dr Whitehead away down the driveway of the vicarage. A police van with open doors was waiting on the road. The vicar had his head bowed, whilst a tear-streaked Dr Whitehead was trying to convince the policewoman of something and kept pointing back towards the vicarage.

Harold turned around and flopped down with his back to the tombstone. With his head hanging heavy in his hands he uttered a few expletives under his breath. It was then, however, that he realised that someone was standing in front of him. He lifted his head slightly and saw two sandaled feet sticking out from underneath something that contrasted sharply with the surrounding grass. It was a bright red robe.

* * * * * * * *

Marigold put down her glass of milk and smiled over at Gideon. "Are you sure you're OK?" she asked.

"I'm fine now, thanks. Really, I am"

The two children sat together at one end of an extremely long polished dining table. Both had hungrily devoured the sandwiches prepared by the woman in the grey suit. They were feeling a lot more comfortable. They had spoken to their mother and managed to reassure her that they were both safe and well and would be home soon. Marigold promised to tell her everything when they returned.

Gideon felt surprisingly at ease with his current situation. He had been traumatised at the vicarage, but his sister's actions in rescuing him had given him a strange feeling. He couldn't put his finger on it exactly, but he somehow felt a lot more confident.

Marigold's mind was moving up into top gear. She was feeling angry with herself for dozing off in the back of the car. This only served to fuel her thinking. She realised that a few more pieces of the jigsaw were clicking into place, and she was now looking forward to meeting with Mr Zarathustra.

A side door to the dining room opened and the woman with the grey suit bustled in. "Mr Zarathustra will see you both now," she trilled.

Marigold thought that she was a bit like a mother hen; the woman now had her arms out and was trying to shoo the children through the door.

"Brush those crumbs off, dear," said the woman, staring intently at Gideon.

Gideon dutifully brushed himself down and the two children followed the woman back out into the hallway and up the staircase. At the point where it divided, near the top, they took the branch that went off to the right and headed away down a long corridor. This again was beautifully decorated with paintings and crystal wall lights.

Eventually the woman in the grey suit stopped outside a plain white door on the left. She opened it and ushered the children into a small room, which was very plain inside in comparison to the corridor. The woman walked over to an intercom mounted next to a large oak door on the far side of the room and pressed a button.

After what seemed like an age, but in reality was probably only about thirty seconds, a weak voice came back through the little speaker. "Are they here?"

"Yes sir, the children are here."

Marigold had been surprised by the change in the voice of the woman in the grey suit. She sounded a lot more formal and polite. There was none of the fussiness in her voice she had used when dealing with the children. Marigold had a strong feeling that she had heard her voice before, but she hadn't got time to dwell on it. The woman in the grey suit had now opened the oak door and was holding it for the children to walk through. Marigold felt an antiseptic breeze on her cheeks as she stepped forward.

The two children found themselves in a very unusual and large room. All the walls were panelled in highly polished wood of a rich golden-brown colour. A soft blue carpet was underfoot, and single chandelier hung from the centre of the ceiling. But what was most strange was the single bed positioned in the centre of the room. Sitting up in the bed, resting against a multitude of white pillows, was a very old man.

"Come closer, please," said the old man weakly, and the children stepped over to two chairs that had been positioned next to the bed.

"How do you do," said Marigold politely, and Gideon followed with a "Hello."

The old man smiled back at the children. "I have been better," he said, "but I feel stronger for seeing you two children. Please, sit down."

The children dutifully perched themselves on the chairs and looked back at the man. Gideon thought that he was the oldest man he had ever seen. His head seemed to be somehow shrunken and was very wrinkled. His skin was pale and contrasted eerily with two very bright grey eyes. The man's hair was pure white and wispy, although large patches seemed to be missing.

"Let me introduce myself. My name is Zechariah Zarathustra."

The old man looked expectantly at the children as if it was their turn to speak.

"My name is Marigold," said Marigold. "And this is my brother Gideon."

Mr Zarathustra nodded back at the children and wetted his lips a little with his tongue. It darted in and out a little like a lizard. "I suppose you are wondering why I have brought you here?"

Gideon nodded but Marigold spoke up. "It's to do with the WraithTalker, isn't it?"

Mr Zarathustra smiled and gave a couple of little nods. "Yes, it is, Marigold. Yes, it's all to do with the WraithTalker. You children have been having quite an adventure, haven't you?"

Gideon nodded and Marigold smiled. "Yes, we have."

She debated whether to tell Mr Zarathustra that the WraithTalker had been destroyed at the vicarage, but she decided against it for the time being. She didn't know what his reaction was going to be.

"It would seem to me, Marigold, that we need to share our secrets. Only then may we get somewhere."

Marigold must have looked a little hesitant because Mr Zarathustra immediately went on.

"As a sign of good faith, I will start. But before we begin, I must ask you this: do you know what the WraithTalker does?"

"Yes, we know perfectly well what the WraithTalker does," said Marigold, resisting the temptation to say "... what the WraithTalker *did*."

"Good, good," said Mr Zarathustra nodding,

"We also know that it works," said Marigold.

Mr Zarathustra immediately got very agitated, and he tried to sit up a little more. When he failed, he rested his head back on the pillows and stared back at Marigold for a while. Marigold wondered whether she had said the right thing. Perhaps she had said too much? Mr Zarathustra closed his eyes for a while and breathed rather heavily.

At length he opened them again and turned towards Marigold. "I can see that you children have been very clever indeed. There is much you have to tell me," he wheezed. "But let us share our stories as I suggested. First of all, the WraithTalker is my machine…"

"But I thought that Dr Black…"

"Dr Black was my employee, Marigold. I own the Hermitage Institute and all the work that is carried out in it. My good friend Dr Black was working under my instructions."

Marigold felt rather uncomfortable with the thought that Mr Zarathustra owned the WraithTalker. She had always imagined it as being Dr Black's device.

"But Dr Black invented it?" she queried.

"Ah yes, Dr Back invented the machine, but I financed all of his research. Dr Black was a fresh-faced graduate when I first employed him. He had some fancy ideas and most people dismissed him as a crank, but I believed in him Marigold. I wanted to believe in him! I took him on and set him up. He and I have worked very closely together over the years."

Marigold tried to take this in. "But you do other work at the Institute," she said.

"Oh yes. I finance lots of projects, but the WraithTalker was the one I was most interested in. Dr Black devoted his life to it."

"And what about Dr Whitehead?"

Mr Zarathustra smiled. "Ah yes, the delightful but treacherous Dr Whitehead. She helped Dr Black with certain minor technical aspects of the WraithTalker, that is all."

Marigold sat chewing her bottom lip.

"I think it is best that we start at the beginning, Marigold. Can you tell me how you came to be in Dr Black's house the day he died, and why did you leave with the WraithTalker?"

Marigold took a deep breath and proceeded to tell Mr Zarathustra how she had entered Dr Black's house after hearing his scream, how she had found him dead, and how she had picked up the briefcase containing the WraithTalker by mistake when the men in dark suits and sunglasses arrived. Mr Zarathustra sat there nodding as he listened.

"You may not know this, but Dr Black was poisoned by Dr Whitehead," continued Marigold.

"I had suspected as much," said Mr Zarathustra.

"Of course!" exclaimed Marigold. "Dr Black telephoned you as he was dying!"

Marigold suddenly realised where she had heard the voice of the woman in the grey suit before. She had answered when

Marigold had pressed the *redial* button on Dr Black's telephone!

"Yes," said Mr Zarathustra. "He suspected he had been poisoned. He had been suspicious of Dr Whitehead and her motives for some time. She had been asking a lot of searching questions about the WraithTalker. Dr Black called this house, and his dying words were to Mrs Antimony, my housekeeper, who of course you've met. Mrs Antimony immediately despatched a unit of my bodyguards to the house; there were some who were already in the vicinity. Of course, when they arrived Dr Black was already dead. My bodyguards then saw you leaving the property with a briefcase. It was later that we realised that you must have the WraithTalker because it wasn't at the house, and it wasn't at the Institute. I've been trying to track you down ever since."

Marigold nodded, thoughtfully. "But what about Dr Whitehead? Didn't you suspect that she had the WraithTalker?"

"Not really, as I knew that Dr Black took it with him wherever he went. It was too precious to him to leave lying around. Anyway, after Dr Black's death we had Dr Whitehead under secret observation. Her movements and behaviour led us to believe that she hadn't got it. No, we deduced that you children had taken it for some reason."

"You almost caught us on the following day, after we had been to the Institute," said Gideon, anxious to say something.

"Yes. My men had been waiting at the Institute, with instructions to follow Dr Whitehead if she left the building. One of them recognised you as you arrived, and after you left they followed you instead, to find out where you lived."

"I'm sorry that we got away from them," Marigold smiled.

"It was of no consequence really," said Mr Zarathustra, although Marigold suspected that he hadn't been pleased. "It only confirmed my suspicion that you had the WraithTalker. Why else would you suddenly show an interest in the Institute and Dr Black's work!"

Marigold smiled.

"It was also because my men had followed Dr Whitehead to the vicarage that they noticed both you and Gideon being bundled inside today at separate times by the vicar. If you hadn't have emerged when you did my men would have entered the building to rescue you."

"They would probably have been too late," said Marigold grimly.

"Mr Zarathustra," she continued, "there is something that I have to ask you while I think of it. Why do your bodyguards wear sunglasses?"

Mr Zarathustra gave a little chuckle and with some effort reached under one of his supporting pillows and pulled out a pair of dark wrap-around sunglasses.

"Put them on," he said, handing them to Marigold.

She slipped them on and gave a little gasp in astonishment. As well as being able to see through them in the conventional sense, there was a little colour image in the top right-hand corner of her view. She could see the black Mercedes outside and some of the dark-suited men standing by it. One of them was smoking.

"The little image shows you what one of my men is seeing through his glasses. All of them have the same facility. Through voice commands they can each see what anybody else is looking at. It enables them to keep in touch with each other and makes some of my more covert operations so much more effective. The little image can also be made to fill the glasses. I sometimes use this to share the excitement from the comfort of my bed, although I was somewhat angry when I saw you cycling away over those fields. I zoomed in to see if you had the WraithTalker."

Mr Zarathustra settled himself back down in his bed. Marigold passed the sunglasses on to her brother, whose mouth promptly went into a little circle of amazement when he slipped them on.

"I have been talking for a while now, Marigold," said Mr Zarathustra, "and I'm getting tired. You must continue with your story. I am most anxious to know why you think that the WraithTalker works."

Marigold again thought about telling Mr Zarathustra the bad news that the WraithTalker had been destroyed. She decided that the moment wasn't right just yet.

"After we had escaped from your men, we rested in the churchyard at St Peter's church. We started playing with the WraithTalker and inadvertently caused a cleaner inside the church to have a vision of a ghost who has haunted St Peter's church for five hundred years."

Mr Zarathustra sat up again and looked most interested. "A ghost you say? How do you know he was a ghost?"

"I will come on to that," said Marigold, "but first I must tell you some more about Dr Black."

Marigold knew that she had got the full attention of the old man who lay in front her. His eyes suddenly seemed to be piercing her very thoughts. Marigold swallowed and went on. "I went back to Dr Black's house that evening, to try and find out some more about the WraithTalker. Dr Black's body was gone, although I now know that the Reverend Orle took it, and so were his notes."

"Yes, my men had taken them to stop his research falling into the wrong hands. Do go on."

"Well, I turned the WraithTalker on and… and…"

"Yes…"

"… and Dr Black appeared."

Mr Zarathustra stared at Marigold.

"Oh, my God," he said slowly.

Marigold paused. She knew that Mr Zarathustra believed her, but she didn't know what to say next.

"Did he speak to you?" said the old man calmly.

"Yes, he did. I mean eventually."

Mr Zarathustra gave her a quizzical look.

"I mean he didn't at first, and he was sort of see-through, but he showed me the numbers to set the WraithTalker code dials to. After that I could see him as clear as I can see you. I could hear him as well."

"What did he say to you?" urged Mr Zarathustra.

Marigold leaned forward and took a little notebook from the back pocket of her jeans. It was the notebook she had scribbled some notes in soon after she had met with Dr Black's ghost. She flicked through the pages, subconsciously chewing her bottom lip.

"You have to realise Marigold," went on Mr Zarathustra, "that this is very important to me. I am a very rich man, as you can see. My wealth has enabled to do many things and to go to many places. What it cannot do, however, is to prolong my life. I am a sick man. I have been counting the days for many years now and I am already well past my time. I commissioned Dr Black's work into the WraithTalker to find out what is on the other side. To find out what I am going to. Or even, perhaps, to find out what I can do to stop it. Can you understand that Marigold?"

There was a sense of desperation in Mr Zarathustra's voice and Marigold nodded her head. She thought she could understand. Gideon was also nodding by her side.

"You must tell me exactly what Dr Black said," urged Mr Zarathustra. "He and I had long conversations about the machine and the nature of death. His work used elements of many cultures."

Marigold's thoughts briefly went back to the disturbing painting on Dr Black's study wall before she went back to her notes.

"He said that the WraithTalker acts as some sort of Communications Bridge between the living and those that have been unable to pass over to the other side," she said.

Mr Zarathustra nodded. "Go on, child."

"He talked about those who were unwilling to make the next stage of their journey, and I remember that he used the word 'journey' several times, and how they could get trapped somehow if they didn't let go. They would be stuck near the place of their death as some sort of spirit."

Mr Zarathustra continued to stare at Marigold, so she went on.

"Dr Black said that, when he had died, he had been unwilling to make the journey because his work here on the WraithTalker had not been completed. But ironically, I suppose, in death he had realised how close to the solution he had been. All that was needed was the correct code settings for the dials. When he had given them to me, he was able to continue with his journey."

"Explain, girl. You're going to have to explain this to me!" Mr Zarathustra was now getting more agitated and his wheezing had increased.

"Well, all I can say is that I have never seen anybody look so happy before. He wasn't frightened about moving on."

Marigold looked down at her notes again. "In fact, his final words to me were: '*Tell him that death is nothing to be frightened of*'."

Marigold closed her book and looked at Mr Zarathustra. "I now think that message was meant for you," she said softly.

Mr Zarathustra flopped back on his pillow and wheezed deeply for a while. Marigold thought that it was best to be quiet, so she sat there thinking. Her thoughts were broken after a while by Mr Zarathustra's croaky voice: "Did he say where he was going?"

"No, he didn't. All I know is that he was very, very happy to be going there. He faded away and walked through the wall towards his garden."

"This has been something of a shock to me, Marigold," wheezed Mr Zarathustra. "Are you saying that we can no longer communicate with Dr Black?"

"That's right. He said that he was moving on to a place far beyond the reach of the WraithTalker."

Marigold sat and thought again in the silence that followed. She knew that she had to tell Mr Zarathustra she had destroyed the WraithTalker, but she first wanted to tell him about the Red Monk.

"Mr Zarathustra?" she said quietly.

"Hmmm,"

"Gideon and I went back to St Peter's church and contacted the ghost there. He's a spirit who is known as the Red Monk because of the way he dresses. Dr Black had urged me to go back and help him. The poor man has probably been trapped in the church for the last five hundred years."

Mr Zarathustra turned to Marigold. His eyes seemed watery. "The more you speak, the more I am astounded by you, Marigold."

Marigold's face reddened a little and she put her head down. "I'm just trying to do the right thing, I guess."

"But sometimes courage is needed to do the right thing. Not everyone has got that. Do go on, Marigold. Tell me about the Red Monk. Have you managed to help him too?"

Marigold pursed her lips together and shook her head. "I'm afraid not. He's a poor unfortunate soul who died with a secret that he wouldn't let go of. I think that he's gone quite mad over the years. He's had nobody to talk to, you see. His best friends seem to be the images in the stained-glass windows of the church."

"And you haven't been able to help him with his secret?"

"Not yet…"

"But you think you can?" interrupted Mr Zarathustra.

There was a pause before Marigold continued. "Yes. I think I know his secret."

If Marigold had turned towards Gideon, she would have noticed that his jaw had dropped and he was staring at her in disbelief.

"And what is his secret?" asked Mr Zarathustra with interest.

"Well, it doesn't really matter now, because we'll never know if it was or not… because… because…"

Marigold found that she couldn't bring herself to say it.

"Because of what, child?" urged Mr Zarathustra.

"Because… the WraithTalker has been destroyed."

Marigold hung her head and Mr Zarathustra flopped back in his pillows.

"I see," he said.

"I had to throw it into the fire at the vicarage. It was the only way I could think of distracting the vicar and Dr Whitehead. They were about to poison us. As it turned out, because the machine was turned on, the Red Monk appeared and saved us. He created the diversion and I'm sure that he also stopped them chasing after us."

Marigold looked down at her lap. "He saved our lives," she said softly. "And I think I can help him, but now I will never know for sure."

Mr Zarathustra spoke aloud: "Paging Antimony."

After a few moments the housekeeper, speaking in her polite voice again, came over the intercom. "Yes sir?"

Gideon felt that her voice seemed strangely disembodied in this large room.

"Come here please."

"Yes sir," and almost immediately there was a click as the door through which the children had entered swung open. The housekeeper stepped quietly across the blue carpet to the bed, her eyes never leaving her employer.

"Fetch the bag out, please."

Mrs Antimony proceeded to get down on all fours in a rather ungainly fashion and her head dived under the bed. She reached around for a moment before dragging out a briefcase. She placed it on the bed and both Marigold and Gideon sat wide-eyed looking at it. It was the same colour and design as the one that was now in Gideon's bedroom; the one that had held the WraithTalker. Mr Zarathustra chuckled when he saw their faces.

"Yes, children," he said, opening the briefcase. "You don't think that Dr Black would have been silly enough to just make one, do you? He always left a duplicate with me." With that he shakily slid a WraithTalker out of the bag.

Marigold had a serious expression on her face. For one moment she looked exactly like her brother. "Mr Zarathustra. We have to go and help the Red Monk."

The old man smiled across at her. You will have to go, Marigold. You and Gideon. I am too old. Take my men. They will look after you and I can see through their eyes."

"Thank you," said Marigold. "But I want you to come as well. We both must talk with the Red Monk. I think it is what Dr Black would have wanted."

THE SECRET

The sun was low in the sky and already turning a darker shade of orange when the Bentley pulled away from Mr Zarathustra's residence. Sitting along the back seat were Marigold, Gideon, and Mr Zarathustra himself. Two of his bodyguards, each wearing sunglasses, were in the front. Marigold had the duplicate WraithTalker on her lap and, as had been usual of late, she was deep in thought.

Mr Zarathustra, who had been gasping for a while at the traumatic experience of getting downstairs and into the Bentley, broke the silence. "Gallium," he wheezed, "tell me what has happened at the vicarage."

The bodyguard in the front passenger seat turned to address his employer. "Deuteron used his contact in the police to alert them to the situation. Within minutes there were two cars and a van outside and Deuteron guided them in. The police found the Reverend Orle and Dr Whitehead cowering in separate corners of the study. Both were quite hysterical. The room was filled with an acrid smoke and the police found the charred remains of a radio or some other electronic device in the fire. As I understand it, Dr Whitehead has been very cooperative. She led the police to Dr Black's body upstairs and seemed quite anxious to be taken into custody. She has been trying to convince the police that she has seen a ghost. I understand that a medical person has been called to attend to her."

"Thank you, Gallium," said Mr Zarathustra. He pressed a button on his door that caused a thick glass partition on the front seats to slide up to the roof. The bodyguards in the front could now no longer hear what was being said.

"Now tell me, Marigold," continued Mr Zarathustra, "just what interest did the vicar have in the WraithTalker?"

"He talked about the End of the World, as if it were coming soon. He said that in the Book of Revelations the dead would rise for the Day of Judgement. I think he thought that if he could communicate with the dead, he would somehow be closer to God."

Mr Zarathustra shook his head. "The fellow sounds as if he's quite mad."

"I'm afraid he is. It might relate to some sort of drug he takes. He was going to use it to poison Gideon and myself. I think he's addicted to it in small quantities. I'm guessing now, but the drug could even be responsible for the colour of his white hair."

Mr Zarathustra nodded, and his tongue darted in and out a few times to wet his lips. "Dr Whitehead must have been completely under his influence," he said. "I know that she regularly went to church. She must have talked about her work on the WraithTalker. The two of them then cooked up their dreadful plan for the poor, unfortunate Dr Black."

"I actually don't feel sorry for Dr Black," said Marigold.

"Why do you say that?" wheezed Mr Zarathustra.

"I know that he's gone to a better place. If you could have seen the look on his face when he left. He looked so happy. He said that the world wasn't ready for his invention yet, and I'm beginning to agree with him."

Mr Zarathustra looked thoughtful and turned his head to watch the passing countryside.

"Marigold," said Gideon, "you said that you have solved the Red Monk's secret. Have you really?"

"I think I have, but that has just reminded me. If we are to talk to the Red Monk again, I need to set the WraithTalker dials to the correct code."

With that she pressed the area over the battery compartment and it swung open with a soft click, its mechanism working just as smoothly as the other machine. She slid the battery holder to one side and looked at the dials. All six were set to zero.

"Can you remember the numbers?" asked Gideon, anxiously.

"Of course I can," smiled back Marigold. "We used our telephone number to begin with, and Dr Black got me to modify the second, third and last digits. The second and third dials have to be set to forty-eight, I can remember that because it's our old house number, and the last dial just had to be wound back by two digits."

Marigold duly set the six dials to the numbers five, four, eight, eight, one and seven. She slid the battery holder back into place and closed the cover. She felt in her pocket for the batteries that Mrs Antimony had furnished her with before she had left the house. Good; they were still there.

Mr Zarathustra had been watching Marigold with interest. "So, my dear, what is the secret of the Red Monk?"

Marigold smiled at the old man next to her. "I have collected up all of the hard facts and evidence. I think it's what Sherlock Holmes would have done. I have then imagined a story that fits everything. I believe I am right, but of course I may be mistaken. I hope that if I'm close, the Red Monk will help me with the rest."

"What is your story, Marigold?"

"I have imagined myself back in the time of the English Dissolution. Back to a time when a monastery stood on the site of St Peter's church. I have imagined the Red Monk as a quiet and holy person, going about his business in silence and with great dedication. I have imagined him as a good man, trying to help the poor of the parish where possible. This is speculation, but it is somehow easy for me to believe having met him."

"So much is conjecture, my dear. What about your facts and your evidence?"

"The fact that the Red Monk is a ghost is obvious. If Dr Black is correct, and I have no reason to doubt him, the Red Monk must have died leaving some unfinished business. It was something that stopped him continuing his journey, trapping him in the sort of world that only the WraithTalker can effectively reach. So how did he die and what was it that trapped him? He told me that he had been 'cut and cut' and he also used the word 'them', so I think it is likely that the poor man was stabbed to death by at least two people, either with knives or swords. I also believe, because he pointed to the spot where he was standing, that he died at the back of the church. And now I must really speculate, I'm afraid."

"Don't start to be afraid now," chuckled Mr Zarathustra. "You're doing so well. Please continue."

"Well, I think that the monastery must have been destroyed during the Dissolution, otherwise why isn't it standing now? All that is left is a few ruined walls. The monks probably resisted, but they would have been powerless against the might of the King's agents. It is only a short step to imagine the Red Monk being cut down by some cruel soldiers, so the question is: why did they do this and what unfinished business did the Red Monk have?"

"He said that he'd hidden some treasure," piped up Gideon.

"Exactly," said Marigold. "He said that he'd hidden the Lord Abbott's treasure. When I asked him about this, he described it as being red and he said it was about the size of an egg."

"Though he did say that it might be smaller, or it might be larger," pointed out Gideon.

"Yes he did, but he wanders a lot with his conversation. If the treasure had been a big wooden box, I think he would have said something like a box or a chest. I have therefore been working on the hypothesis that the treasure is indeed about the size of an egg. It may even be the same shape."

"Could it be something like a large ruby then?" asked Gideon, frowning. "That's a treasure which is red, and it could be the size of an egg."

"Well done, Giddy," smiled Marigold. "That is exactly what I have concluded."

"But did they have rubies in those days?" queried Gideon, still frowning.

"Of course they did. I read on the Internet that some monasteries had become very prosperous. Wealthy pilgrims often gave expensive jewels to the monks who catered for their needs."

Mr Zarathustra, who had been listening in silence up until now, shifted a little in his seat and spoke up: "So you think that the Red Monk hid this ruby? Did you say something about it belonging to the Lord Abbott?"

"I did. The Red Monk said that it was the Lord Abbott's treasure. In my story I have imagined that the soldiers came knocking on the door of the monastery. The Lord Abbott's most precious possession would have been this egg-sized ruby. He probably entrusted it to the Red Monk to hide whilst he kept the soldiers busy or created a diversion. The Red Monk hid the ruby, but as we know he was cruelly killed for his efforts."

"But suppose that the soldiers found the ruby after they'd killed the Red Monk," interjected Gideon. "It won't be there for us to find!"

"No, I don't think that the ruby has been found," said Marigold quietly. "We know that the Red Monk died with his secret. It's the reason that he hasn't continued with his journey. If the soldiers had found his ruby he wouldn't have remained here. He's been anxious for someone to find it ever since."

"So you're saying that the treasure is still in its hiding place?" said Mr Zarathustra.

"Yes, I believe it is still hidden in the place that the Red Monk put it all those years ago."

"But it could be anywhere!" blurted out Gideon. "He probably buried it in the churchyard or under a stone slab. We'll never find it!"

"Gideon is right, Marigold," said Mr Zarathustra. "Wherever he hid it, if it hasn't been found by now it probably never will be."

Marigold smiled at them both. "Oh, I think I know where it is. It might be difficult to retrieve, but I think I know where it is," and with that mysterious statement she started to chew on her bottom lip and dropped once more into deep thought.

The large Bentley swept silently up to the gate outside St Peter's church. Gallium leapt out from the front and opened the rear door for his employer to swing his legs out of, whilst he opened the boot to retrieve a wheelchair. Gideon and Marigold let themselves out of the other side and they closed the door with a dull 'thunk'. Gallium helped Mr Zarathustra into his wheelchair and pushed him towards the gate.

"We'll take you from here," said Marigold. "I think it's best that your men wait in the car."

Mr Zarathustra nodded towards Gallium, and he duly passed control to Marigold, but not before she'd handed the WraithTalker to Gideon.

Gideon opened the gate and the party of three made their way slowly up along the path.

At the door Marigold went straight for the door handle. "It should still be open," she said, remembering back to a few hours previous when she had entered to find the Reverend Orle.

She turned the handle and pushed. The door dutifully swung open. "I want us to stay at the back," she said, guiding Mr Zarathustra to a spot near the great arched window.

"Give me the WraithTalker, please Giddy," said Marigold. Her brother passed her the machine, and it wasn't long before she had fitted the batteries. The WraithTalker, exactly like the previous one, burst into beautiful life; it's blue lights twinkling and glowing in the same hypnotic, mesmerising pattern as before.

"I've never seen it shining as beautiful as that," gasped Mr Zarathustra, who was beginning to recover from his exertion. Marigold and Gideon didn't reply. They were both looking around the church for the Red Monk.

"Where is he?" said Gideon.

"I don't know," said Marigold, unable to hide the disappointment in her voice. "Perhaps he'll be along in a minute." She couldn't help thinking that Mr Zarathustra would also be disappointed if the Red Monk didn't show up. Perhaps he would think that the children had made the whole thing up? Marigold was also secretly worried; perhaps this new WraithTalker wasn't working? She knew that if it was broken or incomplete in some way there was nobody alive who could help.

Mr Zarathustra seemed to be less perturbed. "I'm sure he'll turn up soon, Marigold. In the meantime, perhaps you would care to continue with your story. You still haven't told me where you think the treasure is, or how you reached your conclusion."

Marigold was still looking around the church. "Yes, I will tell you," she said, now giving Mr Zarathustra her full attention. "But there are a couple of things that I forgot to mention. The first is that you might feel the air getting colder when the WraithTalker is turned on. I don't think it actually *does* get colder; the machine just affects our perception in that way. So don't be alarmed. The other thing is that I think the Red Monk, in fact all ghosts, can normally see us whereas we can't see them. When the WraithTalker is turned on, our appearance to them changes. We seem to illuminate somehow, or to have a glow around us. I don't think that Dr Black had time to tell me about the effect, but the Red Monk certainly notices it. He said that the Reverend Orle and Dr Whitehead were also "glowing and shimmering" so I think any living person appears to them in this way. Don't be worried if the Red Monk speaks of you like this. He actually thinks I am some sort of angel."

"Perhaps you *are* some sort of angel," said Mr Zarathustra kindly. Marigold looked slightly embarrassed.

"Come on Marigold, tell us where the ruby is hidden," said Gideon, who was now starting to lose patience.

"Well, there are some other pieces of evidence that are relevant," began Marigold. "The first is something that Dr Black said to me when we were together in his study. He said: *'this room is as real to me as it is to you.'* From that I understood that the room had a structure and a form to him, and he couldn't do anything like walk through walls, although he was able to do this just before he left, when his image started to fade."

"But the Red Monk can walk through walls," exclaimed Gideon. "We saw him walk through the wall at the side here, just underneath those little stained-glass windows. He was looking up at them and talking to them. He also walked through the wall of the vicarage when he rescued us."

"Exactly!" said Marigold. "But there was one wall he couldn't pass through."

Gideon looked puzzled and he even went as far as to scratch his head. He obviously couldn't think of the wall that Marigold was talking about.

"It was this wall at the back!" said Marigold. "This one with the big arched stained-glass window. When I was looking on the computer at the photographs you took, I realised that even though I couldn't see him, the Red Monk had been leaning with his arms outstretched against this wall when I was talking to him!"

Gideon threw up his hands almost in despair. "I still don't understand what it means."

"What it means, I believe," said Marigold slowly, "is that in the period when the Red Monk died, the side wall and the vicarage didn't exist. They hadn't been built."

"But the back wall has always been there!" exclaimed Mr Zarathustra.

"Yes," said Marigold. "Most of the monastery was destroyed, but we know from the history of the church that sections of it were actually part of the monastery. I believe that this back wall has existed in more-or-less its current form since those days. When the monastery was demolished, not even the soldiers or whoever it was could bear to tear this wall down, with its glorious stained-glass window. They left it to become part of the new church that was built on this holy site. I believe that this back wall is as real and as solid today for the Red Monk as it has always been. I am guessing that the side wall, and the vicarage, are just shadowy shapes to him. That is why he came to rescue us in the vicarage when the WraithTalker was turned on; he saw some glowing figures and so he walked over to us, magically appearing right out of the fireplace."

Mr Zarathustra and Gideon both stared at Marigold in silence, their mouths open. The peace was soon disturbed, however, by a creaking sound at the other end of the church. It sounded very much as if a door had been opened. In a flash Marigold had reached for the WraithTalker and removed its batteries.

"What are you doing that for?" asked Gideon. "It could be the Red Monk."

"Ghosts don't open doors in this world," said Marigold, peering up the church and into the gloom of the chancel.

"You're right," said a voice from the shadows, and an instant later Harold stepped forward and came into the light. He was holding a gun.

Gideon gave a little gasp. Out of the corner of her eye Marigold noticed Mr Zarathustra move a shaky hand towards his waistcoat pocket. She knew that he was reaching for his sunglasses.

"Move any further and I'll shoot you dead right where you are!" shouted Harold, his eyes fixed on the old man. Mr Zarathustra froze.

Harold walked in silence down the length of the church, his eyes fixed on Mr Zarathustra. Marigold stood motionless. Only Gideon twitched a little and shifted slightly from foot to foot. He felt the adrenaline rise in him. A hundred butterflies had once more been let loose in his stomach, but this time there wasn't much time to feel afraid. Harold drew closer and he looked grim and determined. The butterflies that had been in Gideon's stomach suddenly came up into his throat. He knew that he had to do something, and it was going to be now or never. The small boy sprang like a cat. With one swift movement he had thrown himself against Harold's outstretched arm; the gun flew from the road sweeper's hand, skidding to rest under a pew. Marigold also moved quickly. She dived down to retrieve the gun, much to Gideon's relief. He was now standing with his arms outstretched next to the surprised road sweeper, ready to engage him in some form of combat.

But it was Marigold who now did something surprising. After dusting herself down following her excursion under the pew, she brushed past Gideon and handed the gun back to Harold. "It's all right Harold, Mr Zarathustra is our friend," she said.

Both Gideon and Mr Zarathustra looked on in amazement as Harold took the gun back.

"I thought he was holding you prisoner," said the road sweeper, rather meekly. "I saw you being captured earlier and then you turn up again with the same people, so I thought you were in trouble."

"We're fine thanks," said Marigold, with some relief. "But thank you for looking out for us."

"We did the best we could," said Harold, and at these words Marigold felt as if she'd been hit by lightning.

"Where did you get that gun?" asked Gideon, who had been unable to take his eyes from it. He didn't feel quite as ready as Marigold to accept that Harold was still their friend.

Harold slipped it back into his pocket. "Er, let's just say that I forgot to give it back when I left the army."

"Harold, you just said that *we* did the best *we* could," said Marigold. "Whom are you talking about? Who's been helping you?"

Harold looked embarrassed. "Nobody you'd know," he said quietly.

"You're talking about the Red Monk, aren't you?" continued Marigold, trying to catch the road sweeper's eye.

Harold looked back at her, completely astonished. "How did you know that? You amaze me sometimes, Marigold."

"You can see him?" gasped Gideon.

"Yes," said Harold. "I don't know what it is about my family, but we've often been able to see him. Going back quite a few generations I reckon."

Marigold gave a little squeak. "You father's name is Simon!"

Again, Harold looked astonished. "If you tell me anything else Marigold, I swear I won't know what to do!"

"Well Simon is the son of Robert, who is the son of Christopher, and so on."

Harold could hardly believe his ears. "Yes, Robert was my grandfather and Christopher was my great-grandfather. Are you saying…"

"Yes," interjected Marigold. "We have met the Red Monk. He told us you were his friend, although he didn't mention your name directly. He just gave us a list of your ancestors."

"That sounds like him," smiled back Harold. "He knew them all personally, but he can't seem to remember my name for some reason."

"It was you who sent him into the vicarage to help us, wasn't it?" asked Marigold.

"Sort of. I just suggested that he might like to go in and see what was happening. When Gideon went missing, I immediately thought of the Reverend Orle. The Red Monk and I have been keeping tabs on his suspicious behaviour for some time now. When I arrived at the church, I was just in time to see the vicar roughly bundle you through the door. I guessed that Gideon was already there. But there's one thing that's bothering me, Marigold."

"What's that?"

"Why can't you see him now?"

"We've been using an invention that belongs to Mr Zarathustra," said Marigold. "It's a long story, but when it's turned on it enables the living to communicate with the spirit world."

Harold's eyes widened.

Mr Zarathustra decided that it was his time to speak up. "My good fellow, Harold is it, are you saying that the Red Monk is your friend?"

"Yes, sir. He is. I've known him since I was a boy."

"And further to that you seem to be implying that he's with you now."

"`He is," said Harold, much to everyone's astonishment. "He walked in with me."

Marigold picked up the WraithTalker. She reinserted the batteries she had taken out a few moments earlier. The machine burst into life and almost immediately the Red Monk became visible. He was indeed standing right next to Harold.

"All this glowing and shimmering. I knew that my angel had come back," said the Red Monk with half a smile on his face. He now seemed calmer, possibly because he was now with Harold.

"Hello," said Marigold to the Red Monk, "It is so nice to see you again. We have brought a friend with us this evening."

The Red Monk stared at Mr Zarathustra who, although he was shaking somewhat in his wheelchair, was far from being frightened by the vision standing before him.

"Good evening," wheezed Mr Zarathustra. "I am very pleased to meet you. My name is Zechariah Zarathustra."

The Red Monk looked curiously at the old man, his dark eyes glistening brightly. Marigold realised with some relief that this new WraithTalker was working just as well as the last one.

"I don't know my name," said the Red Monk. "Are you an angel too?"

"No, I am not an angel. Your angel is here," and with that Mr Zarathustra raised a quivering bony hand and pointed it towards Marigold.

The Red Monk turned to face Marigold and it was her who spoke next. "Thank you for rescuing us earlier," she said. "You saved our lives. Please may I call you by your name?"

"I can't remember my name," said the Red Monk.

"But you told the vicar it was Ezrael."

The Red Monk smiled. "The man from the devil knows his bible, but he forgets that I know it also. I told him I was Ezrael, the Angel of Wrath. The angel who comes at the End of the World to punish the wicked. I knew he would leave you alone when he knew my name."

Marigold smiled at the Red Monk. "Thank you so much. You are very clever. Now I want to help *you* if I possibly can."

At these words the Red Monk became visibly agitated. "Help me she wants to, and she has said that before, and I said that to John, and I also said it to the son of Simon here, and he said that you would be no help to me, but… but…"

"Yes?" said Marigold gently.

"I said it to Matthew, and he said that you *would* help me."

Marigold and the Red Monk stared at each for a few seconds before Marigold continued. "I want to find your treasure," she said slowly. "I want to give it back to its rightful owner."

"I tried to tell the Lord Abbott," said the Red Monk, who now seemed almost close to tears. "But they cut and they cut me. And I couldn't tell him. And Matthew, Mark and Luke and John smiled down at me. Oh, they knew. They knew what was happening."

"I know," said Marigold gently.

"How can you help me?" said the Red Monk, emotionally. "Nobody can help me. I've prayed for help, and nobody has helped me. My friends will not help me."

"Well maybe I can help," said Marigold, not taking her eyes off the monk. "When we were here before, you mentioned that your leg was hurting."

"Hurting. Yes, hurting. And then they cut me, and nobody helped me."

"I think," continued Marigold, "that your leg was hurting because you'd broken it, hadn't you?"

"My leg was hurting, and they cut and cut me. I couldn't move."

"I think your leg was broken because you'd fallen, hadn't you?" persevered Marigold.

The Red Monk was suddenly silent. He looked at Marigold as if he was trying to remember.

"Matthew knows, doesn't he?" continued Marigold.

"Yes, yes, Matthew knows!" cried the Red Monk, suddenly much more excited and agitated.

Marigold slowly raised her head until she was looking up at the arched stained-glass window high above her. Mr Zarathustra, Harold, and Gideon followed Marigold's gaze. The setting sun behind the window illuminated the multi-colours with a soft orange glow, making it look like a heavenly warm tapestry.

Mr Zarathustra gave a little gasp. "Matthew," he said, "and Mark and Luke and John!"

Gideon and Harold looked up at the four main figures embedded in the window.

"You climbed up there, didn't you?" said Marigold, looking intently at the Red Monk once more. "You went up there with the treasure. The soldiers were coming, and you had to hide it. And you hid it in the most brilliant and obvious place that you could think of."

The Red Monk didn't speak; he just looked at Marigold with his eyes full of tears.

"You hid it in the stained-glass window. I think it's hidden in the image of Matthew."

The Red Monk nodded slowly, and he started to sob, not daring to take his eyes off Marigold in case the spell was somehow broken.

Gideon had been staring at the image of Matthew in the stained-glass window. "I think it's in his crown!" he shouted.

Everyone, including Mr Zarathustra, squinted and looked hard at the stained glass. The figure representing Matthew was wearing a yellow crown encrusted with jewels. In the centre was a large red stone. It was certainly a darker shade than the other reds in the window!

"I'm going up," said Marigold, and without a word she had started to drag a table that had a few hymn sheets scattered over it to the back wall. Harold darted to help. Gideon stood rooted to the spot, unable to move. Mr Zarathustra looked as if he wanted to say something but only managed to lick his lips. Marigold took a chair and positioned it on top of the table. In an instant she had climbed onto both the table and the chair and had managed to drag herself up until she stood on the ledge of the window. The image of Matthew was still a good six feet above her. She reached up to a horizontal stone beam that divided the window in two. Hanging from it she swung herself to the left, desperately trying to get a grip with her feet on the stonework at the side of the window.

"Marigold!" screamed Gideon. He'd once more had a flashback to the time she'd fallen from a tree as a child. "You'll fall and kill yourself!" He stepped towards his sister, but realised he was powerless. The Red Monk was still watching, tears rolling down his cheeks. Mr Zarathustra sat shaking and gasping.

Marigold slowly, and with great effort, eased herself up onto the new horizontal ledge, halfway up the window. Using the side for support, she slowly stood up to her full height, her face pressing against the glass in case she toppled backwards. She was now level with the image of Matthew.

Carefully extending her right arm she reached towards the central jewel in his crown. Her fingers felt a raised surface. Marigold gripped it as best she could and started to tug. It wouldn't budge! She tried twisting it and eventually it gave a little 'crack'. Suddenly it was in the palm of her hand!

"Throw it down to me," cried Gideon, who had moved forward to be directly underneath Marigold.

Marigold tossed it down and Gideon caught it neatly. She then crouched down and was able to lower herself off the dividing beam, back onto the ledge below. In a trice she was standing on the floor, breathing heavily. Gideon handed the stone back to her, and she took it, picking off bits of a sticky substance, which had obviously been used to glue the stone to the window. In a moment she was holding a highly polished and very well-cut gemstone. She held it up to the light. Its deep red colour shone like a fire.

Marigold looked at the monk who was still crying. "You have kept the treasure safe. I will look after it now," she said calmly.

The Red Monk composed himself by breathing deeply for a few moments.

"Matthew wants me now," he said. "Oh yes, and Mark and Luke and John. They all want me. I can hear them calling to me."

He turned to Harold with excitement in his eyes. "My friends want me now! I can hear them! It is beautiful; it is like music; it is so beautiful. Matthew and Mark and Luke and John! They all want me now!"

With that he turned and started to walk up the aisle. As he moved, Marigold noticed that she could see through him, just as she had been able to see through Dr Black when he had continued his journey from his study. She almost sobbed with relief. After five hundred years the Red Monk was finally being set free. He paused after a few steps and turned to her with a face that seemed so happy. "My angel. You are my angel. You said you would help me, and you did. You are my angel."

The monk moved as if he wanted to go to Marigold, but something was holding him back.

"I have to go," cried the monk. "I can't stop it!"

"I know," said Marigold, fighting back the tears. She raised her hand slowly and gave him a wave. The monk turned and continued his steady walk to the front. The two children and the men watched in reverence as he walked right up to the altar and stepped through both it and the wall beyond. Marigold sat down and sobbed. Gideon rushed over to put a loving arm around his sister.

Mr Zarathustra, Harold, and the children sat in silence in the back of the Bentley as it whooshed the short distance to the children's house. When the car finally turned into their street, Harold was the first to speak. "Marigold, I've been thinking about the WraithTalker... and I've been thinking about Susan."

Mr Zarathustra gave Harold an inquisitive look, and so he added "she was my wife."

Mr Zarathustra nodded, and Marigold gave Harold a sympathetic smile. "I'm sure she's at rest," she said. "You've never seen her since she died, have you?"

Harold shook his head slowly.

Marigold put her hand on the road sweepers' dirty raincoat. "She must have died at peace with herself and the world. She's already made her journey. That is something to be happy about."

Harold gave Marigold a little smile, his brown eyes looking more than slightly moist.

Gideon spoke up to change the subject. "What will you do with the ruby, Mr Zarathustra?"

"I will find out who the rightful owner is. Ironically, I think it will belong to the Crown, the very institution that almost took it in the first place."

Gideon nodded and tutted, but Marigold had been thinking about something else. She took Mr Zarathustra's hand with both of hers and looked him in the eyes. "Mr Zarathustra, please use the WraithTalker wisely. It was what Dr Black wanted. Remember that the world isn't ready for its discovery yet."

The old man wheezed for a while and licked his lips.

"Marigold," he gasped, "I am an old man. But I hope that I am not a foolish one. I am no longer frightened of dying, and for that I have you to thank. You wanted me to come to the church this evening and I am so glad that I listened to you. I saw the look on the Red Monk's face, and I understand now that there is nothing more beautiful than the journey we all have to make.

"I am also wise enough to realise that I mustn't leave any unfinished business," he said, his smiling eyes now twinkling. "But even if I did, I think that there is an angel somewhere who would help me."

Marigold smiled back.

"I have come to a decision," wheezed the old man. "You must keep the WraithTalker, Marigold. All of us are known only by our words and by our actions. You have shown me, in the things that you have said and the things that you have done, that you are more than a worthy custodian. You will use it wisely and with integrity; I have no doubts about that. And with the ever faithful, and might I add brave, Gideon by your side, I am sure that you will continue to right a good many wrongs. Don't you agree, Harold?"

Harold smiled and nodded his agreement. The Bentley had now stopped outside the Bennett family house and the children moved to get out of the car. Marigold, who was still clutching the WraithTalker, turned back to Mr Zarathustra and gave him a kiss on the cheek. "Thank you," she whispered.

Mr Zarathustra smiled back at her. "There is just one final thing, my dear. It's a question that I'm sure Gideon also wants answering. In the church, when your brother had so effectively disarmed Harold here, why did you return his gun to him? How did you know that you could trust him?"

Printed in Great Britain
by Amazon